WINTER WATER

ALSO BY SUSANNE JANSSON

The Forbidden Place

WINTER WATER

SUSANNE JANSSON

Translated from the Swedish by
Rachel Willson-Broyles

GRAND CENTRAL
PUBLISHING

NEW YORK   BOSTON

Copyright © 2020 by Susanne Jansson
Translation copyright © 2021 by Rachel Willson-Broyles

Cover design by Sarah Congdon
Cover images from Stocksy and Shutterstock
Cover copyright © 2021 by Hachette Book Group, Inc.

Grand Central Publishing
Hachette Book Group
1290 Avenue of the Americas, New York, NY 10104
grandcentralpublishing.com
twitter.com/grandcentralpub

Originally published in 2020 in Swedish as *VINTERVATTEN* by Wahlström & Widstrand.
First U.S. Edition: December 2021

Grand Central Publishing is a division of Hachette Book Group, Inc. The Grand Central Publishing name and logo is a trademark of Hachette Book Group, Inc.

The publisher is not responsible for websites (or their content) that are not owned by the publisher.

The quote on p. v is from the poem "Mean-Spirited Roadhouses" from *The Illuminated Rumi* by Jalal al-Din Rumi, translated by Coleman Barks, Broadway Books, 1997.

The quote on p. 186 ("Death is a stripping away of all that is not you") is from *The Power of Now: A Guide to Spiritual Enlightenment* by Eckhart Tolle, New World Library, p. 46.

The quote on p. 271 about a "cold touch of indifference" is from the poem "Influensa" by Henry Parland, from *Idealrealisation*, Modernista, Stockholm. (Originally in Swedish, translated here by Rachel Willson-Broyles.)

Library of Congress Cataloging-in-Publication Data
Names: Jansson, Susanne, author. | Willson-Broyles, Rachel translator.
Title: Winter water / Susanne Jansson ; translated from the Swedish by Rachel Willson-Broyles.
Other titles: Vintervatten. English
Description: First edition. | New York : Grand Central Publishing, 2021.
Identifiers: LCCN 2021033015 | ISBN 9781538729267 (trade paperback) | ISBN 9781538729243 (ebook)
Subjects: LCGFT: Thrillers (Fiction). | Novels.
Classification: LCC PT9877.2.A67 V5613 2021 | DDC 839.73/8—dc23
LC record available at https://lccn.loc.gov/2021033015

ISBN: 978-1-5387-2926-7 (trade paperback), 978-1-5387-2924-3 (ebook)

Printed in the United States of America

LSC-C

Printing 1, 2021

Don't wait any longer.
Dive in the ocean,
leave and let the sea be you.

Jalal al-Din Rumi (1207–1273)
Translation by Coleman Barks

PROLOGUE

It was the skies, so many, so vast.

The skies above the sea, how they shifted.

Some heavy, dingy-white. Some bright blue, carefree, with only thin streaks of white. Some like beautifully folded crepe across a captivating golden glow, some the dull gray of steel, some a flashing abyss thundering in fury.

The skies, how they arced above the gentle cliffs smoothed by millennia of glaciers, tumbling above the world below, dominating everything.

How they were formed, dissolved, and returned as something new, you never knew quite what.

It was the skies.

And the water.

And the cliffs.

It was everything.

And the people. The people, those tiny beings, who had come to make their homes on the furrowed landmasses. To gather up herring when the time was right, so long ago when they came in shoals so large no one had ever seen the like. *Never seen such shoals.* It was said that you could walk between islands. That it was more fish than water.

The people lived there on the islands, and they set out across that water, under all those skies. And on occasion— not so rarely, not at all—a body fell into water under a sky where it shouldn't have, and that was that. Well, not for the people, of course, but for the water and the skies.

Perhaps there were cries, a name fading into the wind. Cries from land or from a boat, out across the sea.

Sometimes, in the winter, when the sea seemed to become deeper and darker, there was talk of other cries. Cries that came *from* the sea, cries that were looking for land. Cries, larking and luring.

But perhaps that was just what people said.

Perhaps it was just the wind.

1

The eye of the sun, way up in the sky, was shining benevolently and sending down a few rays of light that were scattered just below the surface of the water. His headlamp began to fail; he should have charged the batteries. Oh well, he was almost finished.

Martin let his gaze slip across the rows of suspended farming ropes covered in seaweed and mussels, like a colonnade in an undersea garden. After a moment he reached the last anchor mooring down at the bottom. He tested it by tugging at the rope a few times. It seemed intact. No sign of damage.

Everything looked good.

He turned around, kicked with his flippers, and aimed for the rope that ran along the sea floor. It was attached to the mussel farm on one end and the dock at the other. He was starting to get seriously cold; his hands and back had gone numb long ago, but now his whole torso was frozen, dull as a chunk of dead meat.

At this time of year, in January, there wasn't much going on in the sea. You might spot the occasional little crab scrambling to hide in the sand, or a flatfish lying still and waiting for better days, but for the most part it was so cold that marine life had largely come to a standstill.

Late autumn and early winter were different—the window of time after the summer algae had disappeared but before true cold had set in. When the water was clear and life was still going full speed.

That was the season, when rain, nasty weather, and storms darkened the sky, that it was best to go down into the calm and tranquil realm beneath the surface. He liked to visit just for the pleasure of it.

He found it was the best way to relax, being weightless in the sea and experiencing the world reduced to only what his flashlight illuminated. Everything else vanished. There was simply no comparing it to tropical waters, where you could see twenty meters in every direction. Here, the darkness, the closeness, and the details were the very point.

Nearest the surface were the jellyfish. Tiny sea gooseberries that blinked in different colors if you shone a light at them. And the lion's mane jellies out hunting with their meter-long tentacles: healthy, strong organisms in their element, not the broken, half-dead ones you typically saw washed up on the beach in the summer. You had to be very careful. One time a few tentacles had wound their way behind his regulator; his lip had swollen beyond recognition.

With the darkness came creatures that wouldn't show themselves in the light. Small squid that changed color when they felt crowded, lobsters that left their lairs to go for a walk. Oftentimes they weren't in his field of vision, not the shrimp, not the spider crabs or the hermit crabs either; you had to be on the alert for movement or their tiny eyes, which reflected the light from his headlamp.

He had dived down to take a look at a wall of rocky coral and barnacles. Suddenly he felt something watching him. He turned around to find a white, slightly bluish barrel jellyfish floating behind him. It looked like a small ghost, or maybe an unrooted mushroom or the cloud of a nuclear bomb.

Then he realized that the jellyfish wasn't the only one looking. He was under observation from all directions, by all the creatures gliding around or hiding beneath the sand or rocks, avoiding his gaze, creatures whose eyes were never in the path of the rays from his flashlight.

Now he could see the dock by the boathouse.

With a few final kicks of his feet, he was there. He slowly surfaced and grabbed the ladder, then pulled off his flippers, tossed them onto the dock, and climbed up.

He took the regulator from his mouth, undid all the hoses, took off the oxygen tank, and placed it all on the nearby dolly. Then, his steps heavy, he hauled it all over to the pickup, feeling about as nimble as an overturned turtle.

Once he had shucked the wet suit and hung all the gear in his truck, he coughed the chill from his lungs and sank into the well-worn driver's seat. He started the engine, poured a cup of coffee from his Thermos, and let the mug slowly thaw his hands.

Everything looked fine.

It's over now; everything will go back to normal.

If only he could believe that.

Fifteen minutes later, Martin drove off, his hands turning white against the wheel.

No one was in sight as he left the boathouse and crossed the brothers' land.

No unfriendly eyes on him, not that he could see. Still, he could feel those eyes, their restrained rage, as if they came from every direction—from the house, from the barn, or from within one of the parked farm implements.

They were in there somewhere; he was sure of it.

He wondered how he would keep busy during the three days he was about to spend alone with Adam. Maybe they could make a trip into Gothenburg on Saturday and visit the zoo at Slottsskogen; Adam would love that, especially if they could bring his friend Vilgot along. But tomorrow, in any case, he planned to stay home and clean up the shed and the yard. It would be a few degrees below freezing and clear, not the most pleasant weather. But at least there wouldn't be a snowstorm like last weekend, when there had been close to zero visibility on the road and they'd had to spend most of their time indoors. Maybe he could bring Adam down to the water for a little picnic tomorrow once Alexandra and Nellie had left. Take it easy.

After driving for twenty minutes he turned onto the gravel road that led to the day care. It was right next to the sea, and it had to be the most beautiful day care in Sweden, he'd often thought, once he'd gotten over his initial unease about all the potential dangers that came with being so close to water. The endlessness of it, that the children got to spend every day in this environment—somehow that just had to make them into *good people*, he sometimes thought, even if he certainly but reluctantly knew better.

The children were sitting on a square of logs around the firepit and grilling hot dogs. Martin parked the truck and looked around for his son, finally spotting his blond mop of hair and blue snowsuit. Martin sat still for a moment, just looking. Adam hadn't noticed his father's truck yet. He was living in his own world right now. It was fascinating and magnificent and a little scary to watch, how he was his own person even without his parents. Now he was stuffing down the last of his hot dog and was given a napkin to wipe his mouth.

That pouty, delightful mouth. Those soft, round cheeks. Those eyes that were open to everything, until they reacted to something that was wrong. Often such reactions had to do with Mulle—that he'd been left at home and he couldn't be retrieved immediately, that he'd been mean to some other doll or stuffed animal and he didn't know to say he was sorry; every setback and every pleasure in Adam's life could somehow always be traced back to his rag doll.

Martin pushed his seat back and took off the thick pair of leggings he'd worn for his dive. He pulled on jeans and a sweater and stepped out of the car. As he closed the door, Adam looked up.

"Papa!"

He stood up and ran to Martin with outstretched arms.

"Hi, sweetie," Martin said, crouching down.

They were reunited in a long, hot-dog-scented hug, and Martin felt all his anxieties dissolve and disappear.

"Hop in and get in your seat, and I'll go get your stuff and tell them you won't be coming tomorrow."

It was getting dark by the time they drove onto the county road. Adam sat next to Martin in his backward-facing car seat, trying to fold a paper airplane. A text dinged on Martin's phone. It was Alexandra.

Will you get the popcorn? it read, followed by a big heart.

Martin smiled and sent a kiss emoji back.

*　　*　　*

The small country store was right on the county road and was patronized mostly by folks who lived outside Henån and preferred to avoid the larger grocery store in town. It sold basic necessities and also had a small corner with a few chairs, a table, and a coffee machine.

There was almost always someone around in the corner to exchange a few words with, for anyone who wanted to chat; it was a place to discuss horse-racing tips and soccer results, and Adam liked to sit there and wait. Sometimes a nice man or lady would give him a lollipop or a piece of candy.

"Stay here—I'll be back soon," Martin said. Adam dashed over to sit in his usual spot in one of the wicker chairs. Martin had soon grabbed everything he needed, and went to the cash register to pay.

From the line he cast a glance at Adam; in his lap was Lisa, a little Pekingese belonging to an older woman they ran into sometimes. Martin smiled and sighed inwardly. He knew what was coming. Adam wouldn't stop talking about Lisa all weekend. How soft her coat was, how fun it was to play with her. Couldn't they get a dog too? *When* could they get one? When he turned four or five? Would he be allowed to name it himself?

By the time Martin was finished, Lisa was gone and had been replaced with a small box of candy.

"Look," Adam said in delight, shaking the box.

Behind him was a seriously overweight man in his sixties wearing a tracksuit. Martin didn't recognize him. He leaned on a cane, winked, and said in a hoarse voice, "After all, it's almost Saturday."

Alexandra was sitting on the kitchen bench, holding Nellie and looking through the mail, when Martin and Adam came through the door. A wall sconce filled out the dim evening light, the news streamed from the radio, and the kitchen smelled like parmesan. On the stove was a pot full of risotto.

"Did *you*...?" Martin asked in surprise.

"Don't sound so shocked," said Alexandra, feigning offense.

Martin wiggled out of his jacket and hung it in the hall as Adam ran to his mother for a hug; he showed her the paper airplane and the box of candy.

"You know the rules," said Alexandra, who was more principled when it came to raising children than Martin had the energy to be.

"A man gave it to me."

"But candy is only for Saturdays."

"When is Saturday?"

"Not tomorrow, but the next day."

"But by then it will be gone," he said triumphantly.

He frowned and looked at his sister, who had fallen asleep at Alexandra's breast, a film of milk on her little lips.

"Nellie's sleeping," he observed, poking her cheek.

"You're right about that," Alexandra whispered. "But don't wake her up." She rose to lay her daughter in the old cradle that stood in one corner of the kitchen. Martin's father had slept there once upon a time, and so had Martin himself.

She went back to Adam and lifted him into her lap. Martin bent down to kiss her on the lips.

"How did it go?" Alexandra asked.

Martin could hear the worry in her tone. He went over to the fridge.

"Beer?"

"Yes, please," Alexandra replied. "They said on TV that beer is really good for you when you're nursing."

"Is that true?" Martin asked in surprise.

"Hmm, I *might* have misunderstood," Alexandra said with an innocent look.

Martin poured a foamy porter into a big glass and gazed out the window, taking in the red evening light that slowly lit the sky. Despite Alexandra's playful tone, he knew how tense she was as she waited for his answer.

"It looked fine," he said. "Nothing out of the ordinary."

He ran his hand over his dark, wiry hair and down across

his beard, ending with a few thoughtful strokes of his chin. Then he shook his head.

"I don't think we need to worry anymore." His voice was steady, as if now he'd made up his mind that this was so. "I really think it's over."

"Let's hope so," she said. "Let's hope so."

*A*aadam. *Aaaadam.*

Martin woke slowly. The protracted sounds of Adam's name were floating in and out of his consciousness. After a moment he was awake.

Had someone been calling for his son?

Had it been a dream?

Now he heard something else, from the TV room outside his bedroom door, a more familiar sound. Not wanting to wake Alexandra, he didn't turn on the light, and he set his feet on the creaky hardwood floor and rose from the bed.

He saw Adam standing at the low window behind the TV and gazing at the water, as he'd done so many times at night.

Martin sat down on the floor to wait. They typically gave him all the time he needed when he was sleepwalking, but this was taking too long. Martin stood up, gazing out at the water, at his son.

Adam looked so alone, standing there. So defenseless.

The pajamas he'd gotten for Christmas were a size too big; the pants had slipped down his waist and were covering his feet, while the shirt left one shoulder bare. The moonlight was shining right in his face, spreading across his skin in a pearly shimmer, and his eyes were fixed on a distant point.

"Hi," he said suddenly, his voice so clear Martin almost teared up. It was like a voice from another world.

"Not now," Adam went on. "Soon. I'm coming soon."

Another long silence.

Martin stood still and said nothing. He felt the hair rise on the back of his neck. Adam had never done this before. Did he think he was talking to someone?

Then Adam went back to his room, climbed into bed, and lay down to sleep. Martin hesitated, resisting the impulse to speak to him, to wake him up; he and Alexandra had agreed that they wouldn't do that. They knew the science was out on whether sleepwalkers should be woken or not, but Adam had never done anything to hurt himself while wandering, so they let him stay asleep. Martin covered Adam with the blanket and turned on his night-light, which was in the shape of a sleeping cat. It was a long time before Martin could fall asleep again.

Adam's sleepwalking had begun a few months ago. The pediatrician had told them it was common in children, that it might be a response to some specific incident. A type of stress reaction. Adam's new sibling could be a likely reason, the nurse had explained. During a meeting with the day-care staff, they had been assured that Adam was still his usual easygoing self; he'd always thrived there. With that, they felt satisfied. Martin had also googled the behavior and learned that it could be hereditary. Had he been a sleep-walker as a child? He didn't know, but he'd made a mental note to ask his parents. And to ask Alexandra whether she'd been a sleepwalker too.

Martin woke suddenly at six o'clock, as Alexandra and Nellie were leaving—they were heading off to spend a long week-end in Copenhagen with Alexandra's sister Monica, staying at a hotel and visiting a spa. Monica's neighbor, an experienced babysitter, was accompanying them so Alexandra would have a chance to relax and so the sisters could spend some quality time together and go out on the town.

He received a warm kiss on the forehead and smelled a whiff of magnolia from the perfume he had given Alexandra as a present. His fingers stroked Nellie's soft baby cheek as Alexandra set her in his lap. They were in a rush, and Martin didn't have a chance to mention last night's events. Which was just as well—he didn't want to worry her. She'd had her hands full with the kids since Nellie's birth four months ago, and she deserved a relaxing weekend.

"Take care of yourselves," he whispered.

"Take care of yourselves," she whispered back.

An hour later he peeked in on Adam, who was still asleep, and went downstairs. In the kitchen he filled the espresso maker and placed it on the burner. After pouring a glass of grapefruit juice, he walked out to get the paper in his worn clogs.

It was still dark. The yard was quiet in the morning chill, and soon the open sea would be visible beyond the islet and the nearest skerries. Skagerrak, vast and wild.

He stood there for a moment in the yellow light of the kitchen window, enjoying the serene view. He was one with this island, the sea, the house. Although it had only been his family's country place when he was growing up, he found that it had always felt like his true home. For better and for worse. Almost all his childhood memories originated here.

From the sea he heard the dull, booming call of a bittern. It was an eerie sound. He understood how farmers in the olden days had thought it came from malevolent spirits.

He shivered and went inside.

❦

Martin's parents had bought the house for just under eighty thousand kronor back when they were newlyweds in the seventies. They wanted a place to call their own in his father's childhood home on the west-coast island of Orust, a place to grow strawberries and swim and row out to fish in the summer. It was a two-story wood-frame cottage, sixty-five square meters, with a glassed-in porch and five small but lovely rooms, everything you could hope for. But the older they got, the less his parents left their comfortable house in Uddevalla to visit Orust.

After high school, Martin began to study biology at the University of Gothenburg. He found a small sublet in the Majorna neighborhood and was later able to purchase it, with his parents' help. But theoretical studies weren't his cup of tea, and he quit school after one semester. Instead he got a job at a sporting-goods store just outside the city. A *temporary* job, he told himself, while he figured out what he wanted to do with his life. And then he stayed. He neither loved it nor hated it, just got up every morning and went to work. He spent most evenings at home. He wasn't particularly into entertainment, and he didn't have many friends in Gothenburg. On weekends he went to Orust and enjoyed doing his own thing in the house and the yard. He'd spent all his summers and school breaks there as a kid, and when he was fifteen, he'd started taking lessons at the diving school in Henån, where after a year, he received an internationally valid diving certificate. With his pay and staff discount at the store, he could afford to upgrade his gear, and he went diving almost year-round when he visited the island. His dream was to one day have enough money to go diving in warmer waters.

When Martin was offered a job at the big mussel farm on Orust, he proposed to his parents that he could take care of the cottage in return for living there. They mostly seemed relieved not to worry about upkeep, and he quit his city job right away.

With his parents' permission and the money from selling his studio, he undertook a careful renovation of the cottage. He installed electric heat, replaced some of the 1950s décor in the kitchen, modernized the bathroom, polished the beautiful hardwood floors, and painted all the pine walls white. Once he'd made the house his own, he loved it in a new way. There was something clean and fresh about it, as if everything had room to breathe, as if nothing old was left.

On the day Alexandra moved into the house with him, he felt he had everything he'd ever hoped for. They would be a family. Martin began to plan his own small-scale mussel farm. It took a few years but eventually came to fruition, and at first everything seemed to be going well.

Then the problems began.

He'd met Alexandra one Saturday night at Slussens—a guesthouse with a restaurant that hosted live music in the summer—a few years after he'd moved to the island.

Robert had nagged him to come out that evening. Robert, raised on Orust, had been his best friend since the summers of his childhood, and the one who typically dragged Martin along.

Alexandra had been the one to initiate contact. Martin had been standing on his own at the bar with a Budweiser when she came over and asked him to dance.

He hesitated; he wasn't much of a dancer.

"Well, you can't just stand here," she said with a smile. "This is a dancing spot—you're supposed to have fun. Meet people. Be social. Come on."

She pulled him to the dance floor, and once they'd danced themselves sweaty, they sat down at a table while Robert was busy with some friends on the other side of the room. He knew most people on the island. Alexandra and Martin hit it off right away. She was small, blond, and vivacious—his very opposite.

By the time he got home that night, Martin was in love. He felt so uplifted by their time together that he didn't want to admit it also scared him a little. It had been so easy for them to hang out, to talk about themselves, to touch each other, the kinds of things that otherwise never came naturally to him. Would she still like him once she got to know his true self? Or *was* this new, easygoing Martin perhaps the real him, and Alexandra had just managed to awaken it?

Although he was pushing thirty, he'd never had a long-term relationship, a serious girlfriend, someone he could picture spending the rest of his life with. But he'd always wanted children. Lots of kids, in fact, because he knew from personal experience how lonely, how quiet life could be without siblings.

Alexandra was a librarian on Orust and commuted from Gothenburg, where she'd grown up and where her parents still lived. She had spent several years living with a man, a Green Party politician, and their relationship had recently ended.

She was direct and flexible in a way that seemed to attract her to Martin's quiet, calm nature, to find new paths, like water flowing over bare rock. They saw each other more and more often. They stayed up late, listening to her records and drinking his whiskey, discussing choices they'd made in the past and dreams they had for the future.

She was pregnant before six months had passed, and she moved in with him.

⌀

When Martin headed inside, newspaper in hand, Adam was standing in the doorway and waiting for him, shivering, his eyes bleary and Mulle in his arms. Martin gave him the usual good-morning hug, and then they went inside, lit the old iron stove together, and made pancakes.

"Can I have chocolate pudding on top?" Adam said.

"I know you like that, but we don't have any, we forgot to buy it yesterday. Anyway, you can't eat pudding every day—it's like candy. Tooth trolls love chocolate pudding too, you know."

"Tomorrow, then?"

"Maybe. We can go back to the store, and after all, tomorrow is Saturday."

"So is it Friday today? Or Taco Tuesday?"

"It's just called Tuesday, you know. Today is Friday."

They stayed at the breakfast table for a long time. Adam made art on his plate using jam and pieces of pancake; Martin browsed through the newspaper and listened to the news with half an ear.

He placed another pancake on Adam's plate.

"Did you sleep well last night, Adam?"

Adam thought for a moment and nodded.

"That wasn't you and Mulle hunting dragons out in the yard? I thought I heard your horse whinnying."

Adam giggled and shook his head. He loved their dragon jokes. "No, I just slept."

The big wall clock ticked tirelessly above the kitchen bench. The gray-striped farm cat stalked into the kitchen with a meow that was simultaneously dignified and demanding. Adam hopped down from his chair, went to the cat's dish, and filled it with a scoop of cat food from the metal container beside it.

"There you go, little Fillyjonk," he said, stroking the cat's back gently. "Did you catch a mouse last night? Or a baby dragon?"

A pale sun was shining outside, and Martin hadn't bothered to clean up the breakfast dishes. Instead they'd gotten dressed and gone out to the yard. It was nearing noon now, and they had been out for two hours. Martin had cleared the tools they never used from the shed, raked the frostbitten, half-rotted leaves from the lawn and the garden beds, and shored up a collapsing wall of the compost bin.

A thick, evenly white layer of clouds covered the sky.

"Are you hungry?" he asked Adam, who was at the play kitchen, making snail soup with pine needles and glitter.

"I've got food right here."

"Are you sure you don't want something besides soup?"

"A little. A bun. I want a bun."

"I don't think we have any buns, but I can make sandwiches," said Martin. "And hot chocolate. Then we can have a picnic down by the water."

"Yeahhh, a picnic!" Adam said, his face breaking into a huge smile.

"Great," said Martin. "Go get your bucket, and I'll go fix our picnic basket."

"Can I take my trike?"

"No, you know you can't—it's too slippery in the winter. We've talked about that."

Adam had learned to ride his tricycle just before the first snowfall and was having trouble accepting that it had been put away until spring.

"What about Mulle?"

"No, I think we'll leave Mulle at home. So he doesn't get wet—you know how the waves splash. And we need someone here at home who can watch the house while we're gone."

Adam nodded solemnly.

It wasn't long before they were ready to go. Martin had packed a basket with coffee, hot chocolate, chicken-salad sandwiches, and two bananas; Adam was carrying his red plastic bucket.

Martin pictured how he would sit on the bench and watch Adam collect rocks, as he always did. Adam had an impressive collection by now, and he kept it in an old metal box under his bed. His very "bestest" rocks were kept in a small crystal bowl of water in the TV room. It was a stand-in for the aquarium Martin had promised Adam could get when he was a little older. Instead of a dog, Martin hoped, but of course he never said so aloud.

As they were walking out the door, the phone rang. Hardly anyone ever called the landline anymore, only their parents or the occasional salesperson. Martin was on the verge of ignoring it but realized that if it was his mother, he could ask her to buy some chocolate pudding on the way. His parents were coming for a visit later that day, and it would save him a trip to the store.

"Wait out here," he said to Adam.

"Okay."

"You play with this, and I'll be right back," Martin said, handing Adam an old pay-as-you-go phone that was on the shelf just inside the front door.

Adam gazed at him with his big blue eyes. Then, phone in one hand and bucket in the other, he sat on the bottom step and began to press buttons.

Martin heard his soft voice as he entered the kitchen.

"One, two. Fouw, sheven...Helloooo, dragon..."

"This is Martin."

"Hello, Martin."

"Hi, Dad."

There was a long silence. They'd never had an easy time talking to each other.

"Is something wrong? Are you both okay? Did Mom..."

"We're fine. I just thought...I wanted to check...while your mother isn't around...how's the farm going? Are they growing like they should—the mussels, I mean? No problems?"

"We're just heading down to…" Martin glanced through the frosted glass of the front door and caught a glimpse of Adam's green jacket on the stairs.

"You know I felt you hadn't thought it all the way through when you quit your job to start your own farm. I told you that. Risky."

Martin took a deep breath. He had borrowed money from his parents to get the mussel farm off the ground, but nothing had gone as planned. This criticism was coming out of the blue, and he launched into a long explanation of why the farm was having trouble, without mentioning the worst of his problems. He didn't want to worry his parents.

"It'll all work out—I just need more time," he said, concluding his list of excuses.

"If you're lucky, Sven will take you back. He always needs people."

Martin closed his eyes. *Just keep twisting that knife, Dad.* He felt the bile rise in his throat. He was edging closer to words that would make his relationship with his father even more tense.

"Let's worry about that another time. Adam is waiting for me. See you in a few hours. Bye."

He hung up, then stood there, lost in thought. What was his dad trying to accomplish? He wasn't the type to call just to chat; Mom was the one who did that. Had he heard rumors about problems at the farm? After all, his dad still had lots of contacts on the island. Martin shook off his unease and went out to the stairs, where he picked up the basket.

All of a sudden, he realized the green down jacket he'd glimpsed through the door had no Adam inside. He must have unzipped it and wriggled out. The stiff fabric was standing up on its own, propped up against the step behind it. A gust of wind made it collapse.

"Adam?"

Martin walked around the house, calling his son's name louder and louder. To the swing set. No Adam. To the sandbox. No Adam. He jogged over to the bushes where the hedgehogs usually hung out during the summer. No Adam there either. He glanced into the toolshed to see if the tricycle was still there; it was.

He dashed out to the road, casting long looks in either direction—no Adam—and then he wandered around among the trees for a minute, a few steps this way, a few steps that way, his calls ever more strained, his heart pounding ever faster. At last he set off for the sea. Tripping over roots, slipping, stumbling over stones. He passed the forested slope on the right and continued toward the water.

It was windy down here; the strong crash of the waves against the rocks echoed in his head.

Lightning-fast images flashed through his mind, increasingly panicked prayers that Adam's untroubled face would pop up at any moment, there, by the dock, bent over a collection of smooth stones, or there, behind that big bush, or as soon as he rounded that boulder over there. But no matter where Martin turned, it was quiet and empty, with no Adam in sight.

Instead he suddenly saw something else, down past the big rock they'd always used as a landmark—it was safe to dive there; it was deep there. The object seemed to glow like an otherworldly fruit, something from another dimension.

Adam's red plastic bucket was bobbing on the water.

A streak of golden light opened in the thick dingy-white clouds that hung low on the horizon, like window blinds or a curtain cautiously drawn aside to let a ray of heaven come down to earth.

The light reflected off the gentle ripples that appeared on the surface of the water between the stronger gusts of wind, and it lent a warm contrast to the dark depths that unfolded below.

"This will be good," Maya groaned as she hoisted herself across the bow with obvious difficulty, trying to hold the camera as level as possible above the surface of the water even as she attempted to keep her reflection out of the shot.

Around her waist was a belt typically used for mountain climbing, with a carabiner and a rope attached. On the other end of the rope was Bäcke, holding on and providing a much-needed counterweight.

He was leaning back in the small rowboat, wearing

a thick work coat, lined rain pants, and tall rubber boots, apparently admiring the drama in the sky above.

"I've lived on this island my whole life," he said, "but I've never spent so much time looking at different skies."

"Me neither," said Maya. "Then again, I've mostly lived among skyscrapers or in the woods."

She stretched and placed a hand on the small of her back. Then she put down the camera and rubbed her stiff fingers together; in order to handle the camera properly, she was wearing gloves with the fingertips cut off.

"Damn, it's getting so cold," she said.

"Here," he said, reaching out for her.

She placed her hands in his and let him warm them with his breath.

"It's the changes in the sky that make the water look so different day to day," she went on.

"Is that all? Just the sky?"

"And the wind, of course. And maybe the particles in the water. But mostly the sky."

"To be honest, I've never really thought much about how different the water can look either. Not before I saw your pictures," Bäcke said.

⁓

They had known each other for only a few months. She had taken a wrong turn on her way to see an acupuncturist for her tennis elbow when she spotted him in his yard, a yard full of what she thought at the time was scrap metal and other junk. He was burning leaves and sticks in a barrel, and she stuck her head out the window to ask if he knew where Smaragdvägen was.

"You're on the wrong side of the island," he said, pulling off his gloves; she watched the steam rise from his mouth and mingle with the smoke from the barrel.

"Damn it," she said. "I'm going to miss my appointment."

Instead he invited her in for coffee in his studio, a repurposed construction trailer full of sketches and miniature models and two well-worn easy chairs for them to relax in.

It turned out that Bengt-Åke, or Bäcke, as he was called, was a sculptor and the rusty metal contraptions in his yard were material for a project he was working on, a sculpture that would stand on a square in a medium-sized Swedish city.

Afterward she had returned the favor, inviting him to coffee at her place, and since then they had seen each other regularly. She had even been briefly introduced to his son, Jocke, a long-haired animal-rights activist who was the fruit of an extremely casual relationship about twenty years ago and who now lived in a collective in the countryside outside

Gothenburg. Bäcke often sounded mildly sarcastic when he talked about Jocke and his way of life, but Maya had realized that he had become close to his son only recently, not having been around when the boy was little. Jocke and Bäcke had only each other, though; Jocke's mother had died of cancer a few years ago, and Bäcke had never married—if he'd ever had a serious relationship, he hadn't mentioned it to Maya. They seldom talked about the past—or the future, for that matter—which was how Maya liked it.

But her relationship with Bäcke was developing beyond anything Maya was used to. She had been unprepared for it, and he really had an effect on her. He'd laid claim to her deep down inside, where she was most vulnerable.

She was used to having half-hearted romantic relationships, and seldom just one at a time. She wouldn't say it was out of fear, but perhaps it was a defense mechanism, a reluctance to get close. And she'd never wanted children.

She had simply prioritized other things: her art, her work, things that demanded her full presence and energy.

When she decided to relocate to Orust temporarily, she hadn't expected to have to grapple with the question of true love. Even in the midst of all the warm, fuzzy feelings that had been budding inside her lately, she felt a little bothered that they existed at all. But she had no reason to suspect that these feelings had come to stay.

* * *

In the spring of the previous year, Maya had begun to feel a desire to spend the upcoming warm months by the sea. Through acquaintances she heard of a woman who lived in an eco-village on Orust who was also looking for a change of scenery, and in early May they quite simply switched houses—Maya handed her big house in Dalsland over to Agneta and moved into a tiny cottage on Orust.

It was a little like living in a cyclops. The cottage was only thirty-five square meters plus a sleeping loft, and it had a single enormous convex window that looked out on the valley and the sea. It was equipped with automatic, remote-controlled blinds that could darken the entire house in under thirty seconds.

When Maya came to Orust, she purposely brought as little luggage as possible. She'd felt a desire to scale back on luxuries and open herself up to new experiences in life, and amid the restlessness that followed she had started working out for the first time ever. She began going for a run a few times a week, and...well, it felt good. What's more, she had started cooking for herself out of sheer necessity; over the years she'd grown used to having an assistant who filled her fridge with ready-made delicacies that provided for most of her nutritional needs. Still, she had been lucky here on Orust. Besides Bäcke, she'd found a friend in her neighbor Lia, who was a skilled cook and loved to invite her over for meals.

*   *   *

During her first summer season, Maya learned just how many people streamed in from the cities, especially Gothenburg, to this barren, weather-beaten island community with its fifteen thousand inhabitants—a number that almost tripled during the summer. The sea turned a welcoming turquoise and filled with swimming and boating vacationers; the rocks were warm, smooth, and inviting; the lines to ice-cream stands and waffle cafés were long and winding.

It was a carefree time.

Maya dropped everything, turned her phone off for extended periods, and just let herself marinate in sun and salt.

Then the weeks went by, and when September came, she was supposed to go home again. But another reality was setting in on Orust, a reality she felt herself becoming more and more interested in.

It felt like the sky was slowly creeping closer, settling over life like a muffling lid. The rocks seemed to become more rugged and repellent, as if they wanted to be left alone now, without any human bodies to bother them. As if they had suddenly plunged into the darkening sea, which was gradually transforming into something unfamiliar and mysterious.

It was frightening but tempting at the same time, something she couldn't quite put her finger on.

She had never been interested in the sea before, not like

this, as a phenomenon. Now it fascinated her in a new way that was difficult to explain, and luckily she was able to prolong the house exchange.

It was lucky indeed. Agneta was a translator and painter; she enjoyed living in the forest with Maya's cat, Man Ray, so close to the art school and artist collective in Fengerskog, where there were frequent exhibitions and concerts, along with a café and a restaurant.

Maya herself had begun a photography project that involved taking pictures of the sea—both the water itself and, indirectly, the skies reflected in it. She found that she enjoyed working with the images; they moved through her like changeable weather, establishing themselves in her body like a reminder that everything was in a constant flux, that it was impossible to cling tight to anything—even though that was exactly what she was trying to do with her photographs, and what all photography was predicated on, that very contradiction.

To stop the inevitable passage of time.

⁂

"Are we finished?"

Maya nodded and unhooked herself as Bäcke began to row toward land. Once they pulled the boat up, they turned it upside down on the beach.

It wasn't just that she had met a man, she sometimes thought with great satisfaction, but that she had met a man with a boat. Back then she hadn't even known she would have any use for it, but sometimes the universe delivers before you've even asked.

Later they went back to Bäcke's place, where Maya picked up her car and continued on to her house. They would sleep separately tonight. She had promised to help Lia and her husband, Robert, paint their living room, and Bäcke was going to have dinner with Jocke and his friends in his collective.

"Now, remember not to wear anything made of leather," Maya said with a wink as they parted.

"I will. And I put the meat stew I made in a birch basket," he joked. "Take care, my pearl."

He called her that all the time, his pearl, and she didn't know how she felt about it.

"You bring a shimmer to my life, that's why," he'd said, and in some inexplicable way he didn't sound ridiculous saying it—she didn't understand how that could be.

Aside from Bäcke, the biggest bonus of moving to the island was getting to know Robert and Lia, Maya thought a little later as she took a quick shower, chowed down on a sandwich, and put on jeans and a sweater. She would be able to borrow painting clothes.

They had told her that when they started building their

house seven years earlier and became part of the eco-village, they had made up their minds to grow their own food and live close to nature and adopt a relatively green lifestyle. Maya, who had never been particularly inclined to such things, had been very impressed.

⁓

Lia had been a server in a fast-food restaurant when she met Robert, who worked in finance. They got married quickly and bought an expensive apartment in the trendy Söder neighborhood of Stockholm. After a few years, the frenetic energy and long workdays at Robert's job began to take a toll. He had trouble sleeping, always had a headache, and was often excessively tired. Convinced that he had contracted Lyme disease from a tick bite, he went to a lot of doctors and tried out one treatment after the next to no avail. He took sick leave for longer and longer periods until at last he was diagnosed with exhaustion.

Lia soon realized that staying home alone every day would hardly help him get better. He was sleeping when she left in the morning, and when she came home after work, he was lying in front of the TV, still in his pajamas. Lia was starting to have problems with her shoulders and back from taking on all chores at home as well as her heavy lifting at work.

Robert didn't protest when she suggested they put the brakes on life for a few years. He had grown up on Orust, where his parents still lived, and the two of them thought the island might be a good choice. Lia was a born-and-bred Stockholmer, but she and Robert had spent many weeks of vacation on the island since getting married, and she had learned to enjoy the rhythm of island life. She also hoped that Robert's mother, who ran a small florist shop in Henån, could help Lia get Robert on his feet again. The fact that his best friend, Martin, lived there too was another plus.

When Robert and Lia visited the eco-village, they were overwhelmed with enthusiasm. The houses were near the sea, and everything was so beautiful and aesthetically pleasing. The money from selling their Stockholm apartment was enough to build a house, with some savings left over. It no longer felt like a retreat to move—it was an adventure, a totally new way to think and live.

Once the house was finished, Lia lucked out and got a job on the island as a school cook, and she threw herself full force into various community activities. Robert's mental state increasingly improved during the building phase, and with help from his father's contacts, he got a part-time job as an administrator with the municipality, a role that, to his own surprise, he enjoyed. During the tourist season, he helped his mother in the shop. Soon enough, Lia was pregnant—something they'd strongly hoped would happen during their stressful years in the capital city.

In time, the eco-village developed into a cutting-edge model for communal living that would continue to function even if society broke down.

∽

They were just about to begin painting when Maya knocked on the door—just a little coffee first.

"You want a cup, don't you?" Lia said. "I baked."

They sat around the kitchen table, enjoying the warm vanilla buns straight from the pan.

"You know," Lia said, "I always dreamed of being a mom who baked, and now I am."

Robert smiled and stroked her cheek gently.

"Sometimes dreams do come true," said Maya. "I just wanted to be famous, and now I am."

Lia laughed. "So you're saying that it was glitz and glamour that drove you, and not your photography, your art?"

"Yep, that's right. But you know what I'll have to do to you if you ever tell anyone else?"

"My lips are forever sealed. Have another bun," Lia said, "and then we'll get started."

They began discussing how to go about the job: first put

masking tape around the woodwork, then paint the edges, and finally use the roller on the large surfaces.

"Simple as that," said Robert.

"I'll take care of Vilgot and the homemaking," said Lia. "But he's napping right now, so maybe I'll have time to do some painting before he wakes up."

Robert's phone rang. Maya was paying little attention, but soon she could tell that something significant had happened from his long silences interrupted by words full of restrained despair.

She turned to Robert and watched his face, saw how it slowly collapsed, went pale.

"What's going on?" Lia whispered once he'd hung up.

He didn't say anything for a long time, just stared at them with horror in his eyes as if he couldn't quite believe what he'd heard.

"That was Martin," he said at last.

Another long silence.

"Adam disappeared," he went on.

Lia gasped.

"Disappeared? Where from?"

"From home. From their house. It doesn't look good. They found his bucket in the water."

"Jesus," Maya whispered. "When was this?"

"A few hours ago, as far as I could tell. He was...pretty incoherent. The police have searched the immediate area, and apparently now they're bringing in dogs to search the water."

"The water?" Lia said.

"Like, from a boat."

The three of them exchanged serious glances.

"I've heard about a lot of friends whose kids go missing, and then they find them hiding somewhere in the house," Maya said in a low voice, trying to offer comfort.

"Sure. But it's not a very big house—I assume someone has searched it thoroughly by this point. I have to go over there. Never mind the painting," Robert said. "Lia, you can come with me, right? Maybe we can help somehow."

"No, I'll stay home with Vilgot," Lia said. "I'm sure it would be tough for Martin to have a little boy running around right now."

That was so Lia, Maya reflected. So smart and thoughtful. Always thinking a step ahead of impulsive, emotional Robert.

"I can come along if you want," Maya offered, suspecting that Robert was the one who needed support right now.

"I'd appreciate that. Thanks."

"Give them a big hug from me," Lia said.

Five minutes later, Maya and Robert were in the car, on the way down the winding gravel road, an occasional house on either side, heading for the county road and the sea. Two men by a sauna dashed across their dock on stiff toes, their arms outstretched, with white bottoms and laughing cries. They climbed down the ladder to take a dip.

Maya and Robert drove on in silence, into the forest.

After a while they passed the old mill and continued down the narrow, empty roads until eventually the cliffs and sea appeared before them.

They took a right at Nösund and drove down to the water. Here and there, the road was edged with drifts of snow.

A bit farther on, they saw a patrol car parked at a dead end, along with an ambulance and a few other vehicles. A handful of people were visible through the sparse winter foliage.

Robert drove a little farther, then turned in through a set of open iron gates and stopped outside a lovely old wooden two-story fisherman's cottage. There were two other cars in the driveway.

They stepped out of the car and looked around.

It was quiet up here. Most of the activity was down by the water.

The good thing about a disappearance, Maya thought, was that there was still a chance for a happy ending. But grief might just be biding its time right in front of them.

She inhaled the damp sea air. People were moving around like shadows against the light.

"I'll go in and check," Robert said quietly.

Maya followed.

A cozy warmth was still emanating from the woodstove, and she guessed it had been a few hours since someone lit it. A frying pan with a half-burned pancake inside was still on the stove, and on the counter were two plates with smears of jam. At the table sat a man in his midthirties, with a dark beard and pale skin. Next to him sat an older woman with similar features. Maya guessed it was his mother.

"Robert," Martin said.

His voice broke; it came out as a harsh whisper.

"Martin," said Robert. He went over to embrace his friend.

Martin's feet bounced nervously against the hardwood floor when he sat back down, like he didn't know what to do with himself.

"They told me to sit here and wait," he said. "The police. In case Adam comes back in."

"Sounds sensible," said Robert.

"I want to go in. I want to dive."

"That *doesn't* sound very sensible. That sounds crazy."

"They've got divers ready out there now. Apparently there's a dog that's supposed to go out on a boat first, to search the water. I don't understand how they could make out anything down there. I don't know what I should hope for. If they find something, well…in this cold. After so much time."

He trembled, and the despair held in his body seemed to squeeze from his pores.

"I don't know if you've met Maya," Robert said.

Martin shook his head. They clasped hands, and then Maya went around the table to introduce herself to the older woman.

"I'm Martin's mother," she said quietly.

"Where's Alexandra?" Robert asked.

Silence.

"She was with her sister. They're on their way home from Copenhagen now," Martin said at last. "It will probably still be hours before she and Nellie get here. Her parents are on their way too. And my dad is here, down by the water."

"Is it okay if I walk around a little?" Maya asked, feeling unneeded, especially since Martin had his mother and his best friend with him.

Martin nodded, but Maya wasn't sure he'd even heard her question.

It was a lovely little house—the word *workmanship* came to her. There seemed to be a surprising lack of stuff for a house with two children. Maya wondered why. Was it principle, disinterest, or maybe just a lack of money?

One of the doors was decorated with the name ADAM in colorful wooden letters, and Maya went in. She was reminded of an article she'd read that said the average child in Sweden had about five hundred toys, and a Lego was counted as one.

From all the editorials and discussions of screen time in the media, she'd been under the impression that even the very youngest children had their own TVs, or at least tablets. Even two-year-olds hung out online these days.

There was no excess here.

In the room was a bookcase that held photographs and toys. A puzzle here, a toy car there. A box of wooden blocks and a pile of stuffed animals.

On the walls were pictures of fish and other aquatic animals, as well as a number of dragons, big and small. The bed was unmade, as if the boy had just left it. A rag doll rested its worn head on the pillow.

Maya crouched down and placed her palm against the wrinkled sheet. She bent down farther and peered under the bed. It was empty, aside from a metal box and a few dust bunnies dancing around in the draft created by her movements.

She reached for the metal box and opened it. Inside was a collection of rocks: smooth, round, heart shaped, glass-like. She ran her fingers over them and looked up, gazing through the window nearby, which faced the frozen yard.

It seemed too intimate to go into Martin and Alexandra's bedroom with its big, unmade double bed, but the room next to that, with a TV inside, seemed less private. From here you could see a long way through the trees, down to the water and out across the sea. She saw the people down there, their activity—people on the rocks, in the water, in the parking area nearby.

She realized that she was still holding one of the rocks, and felt its smooth surface with her fingertips.

Adam, she thought, picturing the little blond boy with round cheeks she'd seen in the photographs.

Adam, Adam.

Where have you gone?

Maya went back to Adam's room and picked up one of the photographs. The police might need it if they continued their search on land. She went back down to the kitchen, where Robert was sitting with his arm around his friend.

"I'm going down there," Maya whispered, indicating the water with a tilt of her head. She discreetly passed the photograph to Robert.

She stood on the front steps for a moment, then slowly began to walk. One side of the yard was edged with apple trees and a whitebeam bush that seemed to be fighting a protracted and losing battle with the incessant west wind. Its trunks and branches had turned into petrified figures with gnarled, crooked arms and legs that leaned heavily into the invisible breeze.

On the other side grew deciduous trees and pines that

licked at the ground on a slope. The earth crunched and crackled beneath her feet as she walked across acorns, small pine cones, and last year's half-rotted leaves. Hanging from the tree branches were shimmering strands of pearls—tiny, frozen drops of water, everywhere, hundreds of them, thousands, clinging to the twigs in perfect balance, as if they had been bewitched by the winter cold and were waiting for the moment they would all awaken, let go, and fall to the ground in one synchronized instant.

Down by the water, the boulders rose like ancient, furrowed lizards, forming a bay and leaving space for a small, rocky beach full of rotting seaweed and the occasional washed-up jellyfish.

She counted three uniformed police officers and one K-9 unit. Two officers were having a discussion over a large map. On a bench were two divers in full gear; they were chatting with a few women who Maya guessed were the ambulance crew. A boat was out on the water. A large German shepherd stood on a platform in the bow, its ears pricked, looking down into the water.

A cadaver dog, Maya thought with a shudder.

It was quiet yet very active all at once. No one seemed to be paying much attention to her.

She glanced toward the parking area. There were two patrol cars, the ambulance, a van, a personal vehicle, and a few onlookers. Maya suspected that an alert had gone out on all channels by this point.

She took out her phone and found a headline on the website of one of the big evening papers:

BREAKING NEWS
THREE-YEAR-OLD BOY MISSING

A police search is underway for a three-year-old boy who vanished from his home on Orust, at Ekevik near Nösund, early this afternoon. At the time of his disappearance he was wearing black snow pants, a dark blue fleece jacket, and brown leather boots with green stripes. The police will gratefully accept tips and sightings at 11414.

Soon this area would be swarming with journalists and rubberneckers. She put away her phone and turned toward the sea. Not far from shore she could see wave after wave rise gently over the surface, only to ebb away and disappear, becoming one with the greater whole, making room for fresh waves.

It's so simple for the sea, she thought.

One wave vanished, a new one appeared, and that was that.

She started back to the house. Then she heard a sharp

bark from the water. The dog on the boat seemed to be marking something; it was going nuts, jumping around on the small platform, snapping at the water as if it were trying to bite the waves.

Up by the house she spotted Martin rushing out, his eyes wild, his tall body tense with fear.

"Did they find something?" he said as he passed her, in a voice that contained an abyss, in words that sounded like they were being thrust out of him.

"I don't know," Maya said softly. "But clearly something is happening."

He dashed past her. No jacket, his shoes only half on.

She hurried up and into the house and grabbed a medium-length sheepskin-and-leather coat from the hall. Then she followed him down. Robert came with her.

Everyone had gathered on the little rocky beach and had their eyes fixed on the excited dog. The two divers were already going in and soon disappeared beneath the surface. The ambulance crew brought over a stretcher; Maya didn't know whether this was hopeful or ominous.

Time passed.

The overcast sky was breaking up, and the setting winter sun illuminated the low clouds from below, filling them with gold, a gift in a moment when there was only one gift that would be worth anything.

Martin was in a crouch, shivering, with the coat Maya

had brought draped over his shoulders. He alternately buried his face in his hands and gazed out at the gurgling water, at the people who were searching for his son.

Now and then the breeze kicked up, the occasional icy gust of wind, but for the most part it was still.

Suddenly the surface of the water split as a diver came up. He headed for the boat and handed an object to the dog's handler. They exchanged a few words, and the boat aimed for land.

The first one to reach it was the woman who Maya guessed was in charge of the search. She met the handler and took the object. Then she turned to Martin and approached him slowly, the object in her hand.

Martin stood up.

"Is this…" the woman began.

Martin seemed to steel himself.

And he nodded, a movement without any emotion behind it.

Then he sank to his knees again; he fell.

Before him stood the woman, holding out a winter boot. Brown leather with green stripes.

2

The first K-9 unit to arrive had identified a trail from the house down to the water and on around the parking area and out on the rocks. Given that dogs didn't search for the scent of a particular person but rather followed the general traces of scent humans left behind, some of those tracks could have been left by Martin himself when he was looking for Adam. But no tracks were found leading into or out of the area.

But when they found not only Adam's bucket in the water but also one of his boots, it all seemed clear, as if judgment had been handed down: he was Adam's father, and he had failed to provide proper supervision. Adam had run ahead of him down to the water, where he fell in and drowned. No body had been discovered, but everyone seemed sadly certain that these were the facts.

Martin himself most of all.

When he saw that waterlogged boot, all hope was lost.

His boy was drowned, gone, dead.

*   *   *

The police weren't so sure. Dogs could be wrong, and that same evening they began a massive search effort that included both helicopters and drones. The civil patrol used dogs to search an area of ten square kilometers, looking in outbuildings and barns, everywhere. Then a second group did the same thing again; they didn't give up until the next morning. And when the police felt they had exhausted their own resources, Missing People was allowed in to perform a search of its own.

But nothing.

After the search efforts came to a close, the police returned. There were two officers this time, a man and a woman, and they were not nearly as friendly and respectful as last time. They brought a tape recorder with them, and they began by stating the date and time as well as the names of those present. Robert, who was eavesdropping after being relegated to the other room, was discomfited to note that they were using the word *interrogation* this time. He knew the police had interviewed several people close to Martin and Alexandra; they'd paid Robert and Lia a visit to get answers to what they called "routine questions." But the questions they were asking Martin grew more and more intrusive.

How is your relationship with Alexandra?
Why was she in Copenhagen? Had you had a fight?

Has life at home been stressful since Nellie was born? How is your family's financial situation? Is the mussel farm going as planned?

Martin, could you please describe your exact movements on the day Adam disappeared?

Martin's response to each question was monosyllabic; it hadn't escaped him that he was a suspect in Adam's disappearance. But that didn't offend him, because he had accepted it as the truth. If he hadn't answered the phone, if he hadn't allowed his father to upset him so much that he left his son sitting alone on the steps...well, it never would have happened.

Robert wondered whether Martin shouldn't have an attorney present for this interrogation, and pointed this out to the officers as they stood in the doorway.

"Not this time," the female officer said curtly, aiming a sour look at him.

But no further interrogations followed.

We must unfortunately report that at the present time all evidence indicates that your son fell into the water and drowned. But naturally we will continue to consider the case of his disappearance unsolved until we have a...

...until we have a body.

Those first days were marked by impenetrable darkness, an abyss. The phone never stopped ringing, emails and texts poured in, and Martin turned off his phone; he didn't want to have contact with anyone, friend or stranger. Journalists, neighbors, and rubberneckers had gathered outside the house, and on the road was a whole convoy of parked cars with logos from newspapers and radio and TV stations. A missing child was a media magnet. Martin pulled all the curtains in the cottage. He didn't know whether he was alone or if Alexandra was also somewhere there in the darkness; he could neither see nor hear her. It was as if she had vanished from his life along with Adam.

He didn't even try to scramble for something to hold on to; he just fell, as if to see how deep he could go. There was no resistance. In some ways it was nice, as if he could let go and die too.

The anguish took possession of his body, tormenting him around the clock as he chased down answers and guilt, until someone called a doctor to prescribe him pills and it went away overnight.

Instead he experienced the pain as some sort of reverse phantom pain—he knew it was there; he just couldn't feel it.

*   *   *

After some time—days, maybe, or weeks—a kind of outward reality crystallized, a fog. Then it felt more as if he were inside a bubble or a glass dome. He could see out, but he couldn't reach anyone. Not Alexandra, not his baby daughter. At several points he couldn't even remember the little girl's name, and he would have to wait for Alexandra to say it, and pretend that nothing was wrong. During this time he was acting as a version of himself; he had no idea what the result was like, but it was all he could do. He knew from a purely rational standpoint that Alexandra's grief was no less than his own, but he couldn't see past his own guilt. He didn't believe that they could bring each other any comfort. He didn't want to talk to her. He didn't want to feel better.

He didn't want to be.

There was no reason for him to keep breathing on land like an animal that was still alive. He often glanced out at the sea and longed for it, wished that he, too, would be taken, engulfed, dissolved.

Sooner or later, he thought. *Sooner or later…*

That is where I am drawn. That is the way I am leaning.

The only thing Martin could reach was the sea.

Eventually, Martin noticed that Alexandra and the baby were away from home more and more often. In Gothenburg, apparently, with Alexandra's parents. Because she needed help, she said. He concluded that this must mean he himself was of little help, but he knew that already.

"Take a shower," she whispered before she left one day. "Start with that."

The expression on her face lingered in his mind for days afterward as he tried and failed to interpret it. Was it hatred? Sympathy? Despair?

He embraced the last, perhaps because it was easiest to handle.

They had lost Adam.

Everything is broken. Everything.

That was just the way it was.

He wondered if she would ever come back this time. As if it even mattered.

Friends stopped arriving with frozen dinners and pots of soup. Canned goods kept him alive, beans and ravioli and mackerel in tomato sauce; he lost weight and his beard grew long.

He remembered all the flowers that had arrived, withered, and died. He understood that it must have once been a sign of something nice, something good, but all he could see was a pile of trash frozen in a corner of the yard.

The occasional journalist was still hanging around on the road outside the house, hoping to get a statement from him. His phone was still turned off, and he had pulled out the jack on the landline. One morning he found an envelope someone had stuck under the front door; it offered a large sum of money if he would visit a TV studio to tell his version of what had happened. He wondered which they would prefer: That his grief would move the audience to tears, or that his obvious feelings of guilt would cast him in a suspicious light?

His mother often came by for a visit—a few days a week, he thought. They seldom spoke, and he mostly just watched her broad, silent back moving around the house and listened to her muffled sobs as she vacuumed and made the beds upstairs. He couldn't quite say when he'd last seen Alexandra.

He hadn't even felt the loss. It was totally beyond him. He still hadn't gone into Adam's room, although it must have been weeks. To do so would send him into unexplored, even more frightening territory; he was aware of that. He would be forced to face something inside himself he didn't dare to see. He felt safer where he was now, wherever that was.

Inside of something, something like glass, and outside of everything else.

The fog of pills made his sleep restless; he woke again and again from cavalcading snippets of scenes from the day Adam disappeared, like a TV montage. The dreams he had when Alexandra was pregnant also returned. Happy, expectant, on the borderline of asleep and awake. The dream of a father and son fishing from a dock, having snowball fights, playing Scrabble, or making breakfast for a sleepy mom in the morning. He pictured accompanying the little boy on his first day of school, teaching him to swim, count, drive a car. And then he woke up…

Time flowed on, with no break between hours, days, and nights.

⌀

What was that?

It sounded like something hitting the floor.

Martin, torn from sleep, sat up in bed and listened. His head felt huge and empty, his vision cloudy.

But he was home alone.

Adam must have come back. Of *course* that was it. Martin left the doors unlocked each night so he could come in anytime.

The nightmare was over. Adrenaline pumped through his body.

"I'm coming, buddy," he called. "I'm coming."

He untangled himself from the blanket, stumbled up, and peered into his son's room, but it was empty. Was he sleepwalking again? Martin went to the den. His heart skittered wildly as he spotted the small silhouette at the window through the dim light. He stretched out a hand to touch his son, but before he could reach the dark shape, it flew around to face him and hissed angrily. The big cat had jumped onto the table in front of the window. She stared at him with narrowed eyes, then turned to look back out at the sea.

Did Adam's cat miss her owner? Was a cat capable of missing someone? Of remembering their scent? Their voice? Their pats?

Or had the cat heard someone call out?

He had been so sure that Adam was dead, drowned. Shouldn't it take more than a sudden sound in the night for hope to be rekindled? Would it always be like this? Would he live in a constant state of listening, waiting?

Martin stepped in something wet and saw that the bowl of Adam's bestest rocks had fallen from the table and shattered. He cursed at the cat. Something else was on the floor too, and he bent down to pick it up. It was a small piece of seaweed. Had the cat dragged it in from the sea, or had it been in there with the rocks?

Shaken, Martin went back to bed.

The cat's shrill meows penetrated the bedroom. Martin got up and opened the window, heard the wind gaining strength and tossing waves against the rocky shore.

The next morning, when he woke up, the sheets were

bloody. A shard of the glass bowl had embedded itself in his heel.

When Martin found himself in the den that night, he'd noticed that the view of the water from the window was partially blocked by a young pine and some brush. If something happened out at sea, he wouldn't have a clear line of sight. And that was something he *needed* now. The next day, he discovered that the tree wasn't on his side of the fence, but on the public lands below. The pine had to go, he decided, but he had to make it happen discreetly so the neighbors wouldn't notice.

The night was dark and overcast, and there was a light drizzle as he fetched the ax from the toolshed, walked through the gate, and took the path down to the pine. He hadn't made it very far when he heard a stick break in the grove of trees beside the path, and he stopped to listen. A far-off streetlight spread a foggy glow. Suddenly Martin spotted a dark figure emerging from behind a tree. He was terrified. He started to run down the path, and suddenly everything around him was bright as day. He turned around to discover spotlights and a car with a TV-station logo parked in the grove.

Alexandra and Martin's relationship had always revolved around her liveliness and loquaciousness and his quiet, thoughtful nature. Still, she was the practical doer of the two of them, the one who never hesitated to bring issues into the light and make sure they were addressed.

As she grieved, she felt alone in their relationship for the first time. She needed to talk about Adam's disappearance, discuss what had happened, cry about it, so that at last she could find a way to accept it and move on. Time and again she tried to reach Martin, make him understand that she didn't blame him, that they would survive this together, that she needed him. They loved each other, and of course they had Nellie to think of. But Martin didn't want to talk to anyone; he wasn't looking for a way to move on, since he knew that such a way, for him, didn't exist.

She took the car to her parents' place in Gothenburg more and more often, just to have some human contact.

Early on she would stay for only a few hours, but her visits kept getting longer until she started staying the night. She got a breast pump so her parents could take care of Nellie sometimes, so she could rest or go off and do something on her own. When her mother had days off work, they would take long walks or cook together—comfort food, hearty traditional meals from Alexandra's childhood, no Quorn salads, no smoothies, no chia seeds. They talked and cried. Sometimes she spent time with her sister Monica, and they saw a movie, went shopping. One day she even had lunch with her ex. After offering his condolences, he spent an hour talking nonstop about himself and the latest accomplishments of the Green Party. She remembered why she had left him and chosen a totally different type of man for her life partner. Martin, the *old* Martin—she missed him every day.

Her father had often said he regretted not spending more time with his kids when they were little. That modern men were so smart, the way they took part in their fatherly duties right from the start. Now that he was retired, he had plenty of time to babysit and make up for lost time. Her father frequently offered to take care of Monica's kids, but he came to form a very special relationship with Nellie; he could sit with her in his lap and read to her for hours. In the evenings he played the piano and sang to her when she couldn't sleep. With a heavy heart, Alexandra realized that he was becoming the father Martin could no longer be for Nellie. Her father seldom mentioned Adam, but on the day he gave her a newly framed photograph of her and newborn Adam, she cried in his arms.

Now and then she returned home to the house in Ekevik, hoping against hope that Martin was feeling better and would at least be glad to see Nellie. But he treated them both as strangers, sometimes patting Nellie's head as you would pat a dog, and their visits grew fewer and farther between.

Alexandra's mother had long been nagging her to take Nellie for a visit to Alexandra's grandmother Maria, who lived just outside Gothenburg.

"But watch out," she added. "You know how she likes to control other people's lives. She's a real besserwisser. Before you know it, she'll have convinced you to get a puppy, because she knows from personal experience that's the only cure for grief. That dog was the only thing that helped her get over my dad's death, as she's told me any number of times. Apparently it meant nothing that I pitched in and helped her out for months."

Grandma Maria was eighty-five and in near-perfect health, but she had arthritis and didn't like to leave her apartment as a result. She lived on the fifth floor of a building with no elevator, but she had lived there ever since she got married, and she intended to die there, just as her husband had done.

Alexandra hadn't noticed how big and heavy Nellie had grown until she had to sit down on the landing to rest after making it up three flights. By the time she saw her grandmother standing in the doorway, her two poodles yapping around her, Alexandra was exhausted.

Grandma cuddled her new great-granddaughter, whom she hadn't seen since the baptism, and didn't mention Adam at first. Only after coffee, sherry, and a dry slice of sponge cake did she bring him up out of the blue.

"Are you talking to anyone?" she said.

"What do you mean, talking?" Alexandra asked. "Of course I am. I have plenty of people around me, even though I'm on maternity leave, especially now that I'm spending so much time at Mom and Dad's. And I have Monica and her kids too."

She wasn't about to tell her grandmother what was going on with Martin.

Maria snorted.

"I mean a professional. Or a grief support group, for instance."

"No, no, I can't…"

"You haven't even tried! My neighbor here, Sofia, her daughter's teenage son died last year. Drugs, that's what I think. But in any case, she got a lot of help from a little group for people who've lost a loved one, and they still meet up. I'll call Sofia tonight to ask if you can come along. There are only three or four of them. I'll let you know the time and place."

"But…"

"Now that's that—you've got nothing to lose."

Alexandra let it go; she didn't have the energy to argue with her grandmother. She might as well give it a chance, although it would feel like scratching at an open wound. She had to start somewhere.

One afternoon two weeks later, Alexandra was on her way to a meeting of the support group. She realized that something was off even before she rang the bell in the stairwell; this was no typical therapy group. A business card was taped to the door: *Krystina, certified medium and healer.* Just as Alexandra turned around to go back down the stairs, the door opened, and she was greeted by a young blond woman in a floral-print dress.

"Alexandra, I presume. Welcome, the others are already here. I'm Krystina. Come in, come in. Help yourself to a cup of tea in there. I just have to take care of one thing."

The apartment was small and dark. There were four other women, two around Alexandra's age and the others around sixty, she guessed. Each introduced herself with her first name and whom she'd lost: one had been widowed, one had a late miscarriage, one had lost her elderly mother, and then Sofia, who, like Alexandra, was grieving a child. The other four obviously knew each other already, and Alexandra felt uncomfortable, like an outsider, but she couldn't quite summon the will to leave. Once they'd finished their rooibos tea, Krystina invited them to sit around a table in an adjoining room. A lit candle was on the table, aligning perfectly with the cliché. After just a few minutes of silence, she began to tell them that she had contacted someone from the other side.

"It's a little boy. Just a few years old. And I see water, lots of water…"

Alexandra leaped to her feet and ran for the door, grabbing her coat as she went and hurrying down the stairs, to the street, where she vomited violently.

Surely her grandmother must have told them about Adam?

✑

Robert's friend Maya had flickered through Martin's field of vision often enough that she eventually stuck in his consciousness—unlike many others who had come and gone since the disaster: police officers, psychologists, friends of friends, all kinds of people. Everyone who wanted to help. Or just find out what it felt like when the worst happened. Was there any getting over such a loss? Could you tell by looking at someone whether he was guilty or innocent?

Maya had been...a little obstinate, he thought at first. When other visitors became few and far between, she kept knocking at his door. Coming by with treats even though he never ate anything. He hadn't had any reason to object, so he'd allowed her to push her way in and drink her coffee.

She didn't seem to demand anything in return.

Sometimes they played cards or chess. Once she brought a thousand-piece puzzle and set it up on the table on the sunporch. Then she sat there for half the day, hmming and turning the pieces this way and that as he did other things—or, rather, nothing.

After a while he sat down next to her and began to search through the confusing pieces of sky blue or grass green that were meant to fit in with the hundreds of other apparently identical pieces.

He felt more and more comfortable in her presence as he began to feel that he didn't have to give anything at all, or even respond when she spoke to him. She seemed satisfied either way; she never did anything practical that made his life easier, but sometimes she would suddenly put on a song and comment on the guitar riffs in the third verse.

As time went on, she spoke more and more. Not about herself or about him—she never did that—but about anything and everything else. What the weather report said, what was going on in the world, things she'd read or heard. Never anything that would upset him. He just let it wash over him, snapping up a piece of it here or there, but she never asked for his opinion on anything, nor did he have one.

And then one day, she began to tell him about a TV show she was watching on Netflix. Later he came to realize that she was purposefully describing it episode by episode, one for each visit. It was exciting, and once he had started to listen actively, he couldn't stop.

At last he noticed a feeling that was almost like...not happiness, definitely not, but something that rose above his general numbness. Anticipation.

Eventually she did ask him some questions as well. In time, he realized something was bothering her, that she couldn't stop wondering if Adam might not have drowned but had been taken. Was she trying to provoke a reaction in him? Fury? *Who the hell do you think you are, coming here and trying to keep my false hope alive?* Or hope? But at first, he felt neither. There was no reaching him when it came to Adam. He just let her talk, not because she was giving him any sort of hope that his son might be alive after all, but because he had come to appreciate her presence a bit more than her absence.

Which was probably because in her company, he was given permission to be exactly who he was. Precisely as pointless and nonexistent as he felt. So full of self-hatred. And also because her stories helped pass the time.

Until we have a body.

It was as though the boy's shoe became the conclusive evidence that he had fallen into the water and vanished.

Which could, of course, be the case.

But Maya realized she didn't want to accept that idea. Or, more accurately, she thought that everyone involved had accepted it a little too readily. Sure, the currents could sweep a tiny body away in no time; it could be a hundred meters below the surface and halfway to Denmark by this point, but in the end, there was still the fact that no body had been found.

As far as she knew, there was still an open investigation into a possible kidnapping, but it hadn't led anywhere. And if someone had taken Adam, surely they wouldn't have been so stupid as to toss the bucket and a shoe into the water, right?

The published photographs of Martin sneaking around

in the dark of night, ax in hand and confusion on his face, had certainly done nothing to make him seem less a suspect in the eyes of the public.

"How did they manage to make poor Martin look like Jack Torrance in *The Shining*?" an upset Maya had exclaimed to Bäcke.

"It must have been like Christmas morning for that news outlet when he came running out like that. Do you think the police seriously suspect Martin of hurting Adam?" Bäcke wondered.

"No, I really don't. But if they eventually come to the conclusion that Adam drowned, there's some chance he'll be charged with involuntary manslaughter. It's considered gross negligence to leave such a small child unsupervised."

In addition, it was still unclear who had been terrorizing the family in various ways up until a few months before Adam's disappearance.

Robert and Lia had first mentioned it on the evening after Adam went missing, as they were all drinking wine at their eco-house made of wood, mud, and linen.

Robert had been crying. Martin was a childhood friend, and their children had been born right around the same time. They'd gone through paternity leave together and followed the development of each other's sons during those first years.

"They were supposed to grow up together," he sobbed as Lia stroked his back slowly. "Now that's all gone."

Darkness had fallen outside the windows, enclosing everything in soft velvet, like an act of mercy.

"I heard about the criminal investigation," Maya said. "Do you know what it's based on?"

"It must be the sabotage, the call, the letters," said Robert, taking out a handkerchief and blowing his nose.

The look Maya gave him encouraged him to go on.

"When Martin started his mussel farm, he got permission from the municipality to use a boathouse and a small strip of the beach nearby to store his equipment. That's a few kilometers from where he lives, in a place where it's deep enough, not so far offshore, to hang the farming ropes."

"So what was the problem?"

"It turned out the family who lives right next to that spot had always used the boathouse and the beach as their own. The two brothers who still live there weren't too happy about Martin's little stunt."

"Which is understandable, I suppose," said Maya.

"Sure. And Martin isn't the smoothest in that sort of situation either," said Robert.

"What do you mean?"

"He can be…a little rigid. Once he had permission to

use the space, that was that, period. Like, no matter what had gone on there in the past."

"So what happened?" Maya asked.

"These two brothers were constantly getting after him, every time he went there or whenever they ran into each other in town. Telling him to move his stuff, in pretty unpleasant terms. He refused. Then some of his stuff was broken, some disappeared. Eventually they started calling his cell phone. At least, he thought it was them. He would get calls from a blocked number in the middle of the night, and no one on the other end said anything. After that he received some threatening letters too, as I recall."

He took a sip of wine.

"But Martin didn't give in, and in the end nothing else happened. Until a few months ago, when someone cut the lines that anchored his farm. A fisherman found it floating in the shipping channel."

"Couldn't the rope have broken?"

"The ends weren't ragged at all. They'd been cut. I saw it myself—there was no question. But I think things had calmed down recently."

"What else do you know about those brothers?" Maya asked.

Lia shook her head.

"Not much," she said. She seemed to be trying to catch Robert's eye to see if he agreed. "They must be ten years younger than us, so we've never moved in the same circles. But, oh…I know they live together and do a little bit of farming. And that they…like, mess around with cars and stuff. People say they were kind of wild as teenagers. Their last name is Johansson, by the way."

"That farm is their childhood home," Robert added. "Their father was found hanged in the forest a few years ago. I wonder if it was one of the brothers who found him."

Lia looked down at the table.

"The mother was never in the picture, as far as I know. I expect they haven't had an easy life."

Later, as Maya walked the short distance back to her house, she thought about how much she would miss kind-hearted, bun-baking Lia, so unlike herself, once she moved back to the forest again. It wasn't the only thing she would miss.

⚬

When she became part of the eco-village, she had immediately taken on a balancing act, one that seemed to be working well so far: finding that sweet spot between being part of a community and not allowing herself to be drawn too deeply into local concerns.

The most long-term projects, of course, fell away for natural reasons; for instance, there had been a lot of talk and meetings about a future common space that might eventually be created out of an old barn down by the road. A simple pub that could also be rented out for classes or parties. Perhaps there would also be a few small rooms with beds for guests of residents. She didn't get involved in any of this, or in discussions about the maintenance of the common wastewater treatment facility, or in the question of whether residents' guests should be allowed to book the sauna by the sea.

On the other hand, she did want to be useful, or at least visible, on community cleanup or building days, although she knew she was far from indispensable when it came to that kind of practical activity.

That was probably what she had been most afraid of before moving here—that she wouldn't have time for her work. But in the end, she ventured to trust that there was no need to grow her own vegetables, knit ragg socks, or keep chickens. The house was a house like any other, even though it was built entirely of natural materials and in some magical way kept itself warm without any external heating system. She got her electricity from the village's own solar- and wind-power installations and had a toilet that separated liquids and solids, which went straight to the village's wastewater facility, but there wasn't anything noticeably different about it as long as everything was working properly—which was just what it seemed to do.

The smaller houses in the eco-village shared showers, a laundry room, and some other common spaces, and that posed no problem for her, although she missed her long, lavender-scented bubble baths in the evenings. When she took over the house, she had promised to tend to the small allotment garden that went with it, and early in her first spring some greenery had come up that Maya, with the help of Google, managed to identify as rhubarb, mint, and chives. She'd never expected to find satisfaction in watching something grow, in tending the earth, but later in the summer, when she harvested the first of the lettuce she'd sown herself, she felt an almost ridiculous amount of joy. Maybe she could do something about the garden when she moved back to her own house again.

The view down to the sea from her cyclops window was fantastic.

In the days following Adam's disappearance, Maya paid regular visits to Martin's house. She "was just passing by," as she said, and always brought along vanilla buns or cinnamon rolls from Lia or the bakery, treats she ended up eating by herself. Sometimes she brought TV dinners and stuck them in the freezer, to no reaction from Martin.

Maybe it was the presumed drowning that woke in her a

desire to investigate—for over twenty years, she had worked part-time as a police photographer. But it had been a long time now. These days, she was trying to convince herself that she wasn't a busybody, that she was interested in this case out of sheer concern for all involved. She didn't want to admit that she was fascinated by crime and violence— murder, manslaughter, assault—and that she missed the excitement of her close work with investigators. Even before she got that first job with the police in Karlstad, when she was younger, she had felt at home at the station there. Her mother was a police officer.

Now she couldn't quite let go of what had happened to Adam, not least because she wanted to know more about what had occurred before he disappeared. Besides, Robert had asked if she would consider looking in on Martin during the day occasionally if she had time, and that served as an excuse. Robert had come to understand that Alexandra was seldom home, and if her car was in the driveway, Maya could always just keep driving.

Most of the time Maya and Martin sat at the big gateleg table in Martin's kitchen. Maya made coffee and put out the baked goods and then took out her deck of cards, because it always, *always* worked for her. She didn't understand why card games played such a hidden role in Swedish social life. Or maybe they didn't; maybe they were just such a self-evident part of it that no one even needed to bring it up.

"Want to play something?"

Typically he said no whenever she asked, and she would play solitaire while he watched. When he did say yes, they mostly played poker or skitgubbe. He sometimes seemed to be sucked in by the game, and she liked to see that, to see him relax into an activity. The best was when they played chess. Practically speaking, they could take as much time as they liked between turns, and still no one had to say a word. She also congratulated herself on the lucky accident of having started to tell him about the historical TV series she liked to follow; after a while she could tell that he was coming out of his fog and really listening.

Maya had heard from Robert that diving was Martin's greatest interest and that in the past he could talk for hours about underwater life. Maybe that was a topic that would get him to open up, she thought.

"Can you tell me about diving?" she asked one evening when he'd accepted her offer of a game of chess and she had just let out a low chuckle and taken his knight with a pawn. "I've never had much of a relationship with the sea myself. It's always seemed…foreign somehow. But of course, I've had very little to do with it."

"I guess for me, I've been fascinated with it from the start," said Martin.

"Fascinated how?"

"On all levels, I think."

"Such as…?"

He shrugged.

"Biologically. Politically. Experience-wise. I'm fascinated by the marine plants that make up the bottom of the food chain and are eaten by the invertebrates that become food for small fish and shellfish… which, in the end, attract larger predators. By the way the cell, the original component of life, has adapted to salt water."

He paused.

"Sometimes I think it's why we find it so easy to toss our trash in the water. We sort of have this image of the sea as endless, like outer space, and we think that our crap just disappears—like, a few drums of PCBs more or less, what does it matter?"

"Well, we know all of that nowadays, but from that to going down into the darkness…"

Once he began to talk about his diving, it was as if Maya saw a new Martin, or maybe this was the Martin he had been before she met him. Gone were the monosyllabic replies; he described the beauty under the sea dreamily and eloquently: the coral and barnacles, the jellyfish and crabs, the sunlight filtering through the water.

"Can you dive in the winter, here on the island?" she wondered. "That must be pretty damn cold."

He nodded. "You sure can, if you have the right equipment. And oftentimes you get the best visibility in early winter, because there's not as much algae or other particles in the water."

"How is your mussel farm doing, by the way?" Maya asked, figuring she might as well take the opportunity to ask while he was feeling talkative.

"My mussel farm?" he said as he took in the chessboard. "Oh, it's gone now. I think Dad brought it ashore. That's the end of that."

"How long had you had it?"

"I guess it wasn't quite a year. Nothing much came of it. Never really got it off the ground."

She could smell his body odor when he raised his arm to move a piece, a whiff of stuffiness, of age that was as yet invisible.

"What did you do before you were an entrepreneur?"

"I worked at a different mussel farm. For a bigger company with lots of employees and installations all around Orust."

He moved his queen halfway across the board, finally putting her king in check.

"And what did they think when you started your own farm? Of having competition?"

"I don't think they were all that worried," he said, almost chuckling. "Sven, the owner, he's an old friend of mine and Dad's, and he helped me start my company. He's an environmentalist. He's of the opinion that it can only be a good thing that more and more folks are becoming interested in mussel farming."

"So mussels are good for the environment?"

Martin nodded. "They filter harmful particles from the water. Combat overfertilization and all that."

"But there were other people who weren't so happy you had started your own farm?"

He looked at her.

"Oh. So you've heard about that."

"Do you know what the police have done about it?"

"Last I heard, the brothers had been brought in for questioning. Not as suspects or anything, just…for informational purposes, I think they called it. About the sabotage. I've been down to the station a few times about this, but apparently a child had to disappear before they did anything about it."

"They think there could be a connection to Adam going missing?"

Martin shrugged.

"They're not ruling anything out, as they say. Sabotage is one thing, but to me it seems pretty clear what happened to Adam. It was no one's fault but my own."

He moved his knight.

"Checkmate," he said, pushing the board away and looking right at her.

"So what did they say, the brothers?" Maya asked. "About the property damage?"

"Naturally, they denied everything. Apparently they claimed to have seen a boat out the night the lines were cut. A boat they didn't recognize."

"And you think they were lying?"

"I don't know. I've always assumed it was them."

"I heard you received some nasty letters. Do you still have them?"

"No, I tossed them—except the last one. That one, I gave to the police. By then I'd had enough."

Maya nodded and tried to hide her disappointment.

"But I did take a picture of it first."

"Can I see?"

"Sure."

Martin disappeared for a moment and returned with his phone. It was off, and Maya guessed he hadn't used it for a while. After he found the charger and plugged it in, he handed the phone to her and showed her what appeared to be a page of college-ruled A5 notebook paper. Next to it was a pale blue envelope.

THIS IS YOUR FINAL WARNING, the paper read in black marker.

"Yikes," Maya muttered. "That almost looks kind of childish."

"Maybe. But it didn't feel that way when we got it.

Alexandra especially was very upset. And she was pregnant at the time too."

"I understand," Maya said, taking another look. "Nothing to suggest what the warning was about?"

Martin shook his head.

"But it wasn't that hard to figure out—the brothers had made it pretty clear what they wanted me to stop doing."

"Was there any writing on the envelopes? Did they have stamps?" Maya wondered.

"No. Someone had just stuck them in the mailbox out by the road."

"And then someone cut the lines?"

"Exactly. That was in October, if I remember correctly. November, maybe."

"And nothing has happened since?"

"Right."

They sat in silence.

"What kind of stuff were you keeping down by the water, anyway?" she asked at last.

"There are still ropes and dropper lines there, as far as I know. Buoys. Nets. Plus the rowboat."

She gazed past the counter and out the window. The shiny, naked trees were like sharp spears against the paler evening sky.

"I can go get it for you," she said.

"You? Why would you do that?"

"Because I want to show a fellow human in need that I can do other things besides eat buns and play cards."

He looked down at the table.

"Okay. Sure. I'd be grateful for that. Do you have a trailer hitch on your car? Otherwise you can take mine. I have a trailer too."

"Good to know. I'll pick it all up when the time is right. I can't say when that will be, but I'll try to get to it as soon as I can, so you can stop worrying about it."

He let out what sounded like a laugh.

"I think that's actually the problem. That I already stopped worrying about it, even though I shouldn't have. That I stopped worrying about everything."

Silence.

"They say I have to talk to the doctor again," Martin said at last. "That I'm sick."

For the first time, Maya went over and put her arms around him. It wasn't really a hug, given how slack he felt; it was more as if she were embracing a jumble of body parts.

She thought about the fact that this man had a wife and a brand-new little baby, but it seemed like he had already checked out, as if he were on his way out of life. As if life were on its way out of his body. But today, for the first time, they had had a real conversation. An almost entirely normal one, with questions and answers. It felt like this might be the start of something after all. Maybe they had been wrong. Maybe they shouldn't have left him on his own; that was showing misguided consideration. Instead, they should force him to react, to come out of his paralyzed state and live his grief.

"How…how are you all doing?" Maya whispered. She imagined that so many people must be wondering the same thing, but maybe no one was asking. To keep from hurting him, or maybe just because the answer was so clear.

"Who?" Martin responded.

He gazed at her with large, empty eyes.

It looked as though for the life of him, he couldn't figure out whom she was talking about.

Maya couldn't get Martin's lyrical descriptions of underwater life out of her head. Was there a whole new world down there for her to experience? And what could be more logical than delving below the surface where her work was currently located? As if art had anything to do with logic, she corrected herself. The problem was, she would need to be able to dive. Could you learn how if you were over fifty?

There was a company in Svineviken where you could hire divers, and there would likely be someone there who could answer her questions. It was a beautiful day, so Maya took a chance and drove there; she could run some errands along the way.

This time of year there weren't many people around the bay. After wandering for a while she found a guy fiddling with an engine, not looking too busy, outside the company office. He wore a name tag that read *Mattias*. They took a little walk down to the water behind the building as they chatted.

"All you need is to be healthy—you have to have a clean bill of health or a physical before you can take a course," he explained as he fished a half-smoked cigarette from his breast pocket and lit it with an old Zippo.

"What about my age? Would I be able to learn to dive?"

"Definitely," he said, studying her. "Haven't you heard of Leni Riefenstahl? She lied about her age when she was eighty so she could get certified. Then she became a great underwater photographer."

"Wow, she sure had a lot of hobbies, that woman." Maya gazed out at the empty beach and the calm water. "It's so peaceful here."

Mattias nodded. "Yes, but time moves quickly, and soon this place will be chock-full of summer tourists and those things." He nodded at a collection of Jet Skis lined up under tarps near the dock. "And then it will be a whole different kind of energy down here."

"Oh yes, I remember those things from last year. They make a hell of a racket. Don't people get angry?" Maya wondered.

"We have a very active Jet Ski club here. And a successful one—this year we're going for gold in the European championships in Zagreb," he said proudly, "so there will be an intense training period. But most of the people zooming around for fun in the bays are tourists, and after all, the season isn't that long."

"But the people with houses along the water must complain, right?"

"Sure. We get a lot of phone calls and nasty letters during the season, and we're always after our members to take it easy near the beaches. Last year someone even sent a threatening letter, but we do actually have permission to be here."

Maya's ears pricked up. "What was the threat?"

"It wasn't clear. Something unpleasant would happen if we didn't stop, was all. We didn't take it very seriously at first. But just a few weeks later, there was an accident during one of our races."

"What happened?"

"This guy was supposed to turn and go around one of the buoys in the course, but instead he went straight, ran into a shoal, and was thrown from the Jet Ski. It was a serious crash, but he got lucky—he just broke an arm and got a little banged up. He claimed that something was wrong with the steering, that someone must have messed with it. So that's when we filed a police report and handed over the letter, which we happened to have kept. Usually we toss that sort of thing right away."

"What did the police say?"

"They closed the case pretty quickly." He shrugged. "They said there was no way to prove a link between the letter and the accident. And I suppose they were right. The guy might have just hit the gas by accident and needed something to blame it on."

"And you haven't received any more letters? Was this one postmarked from the island, by the way?"

"No, we never got any more like that, just the typical complaints. Someone had put it right in the club mailbox. There was no address."

"Do you remember what it looked like?"

"No, I guess it was just a regular old piece of paper, not very big, and someone had written on it with black marker. Why do you ask?"

"Just curious," Maya said, thanking him for all his help.

"Feel free to get in touch again if there's anything else," he said.

Maya got the impression that he didn't have many people to talk to at the diving company this time of year.

After running her errands, she went to a café on Hamntorget and ordered coffee and a piece of chocolate cake with whipped cream. She thought about what Mattias had said. *If* the Jet Ski accident and the letter were related, and *if* it was the same person who'd sent Martin's letter...well, maybe they hadn't taken the letter writer seriously enough.

She had to find out what the letter sent to the Jet Ski club looked like. She googled the closest police station, which turned out to be in Stenungsund, but its office hours were over for the day.

On her way home she stopped at the bookstore to look for a few books about underwater photography.

What did Martin do all day? Mostly lay in bed. Dozing. He got up around lunchtime, fixed something to eat, sat in front of the TV, ate again. He sometimes went out to putter in the yard or fed the cat if he remembered to. Collapsed in front of the TV again—he still couldn't recall a single show he'd seen, and his thoughts flapped around everywhere and nowhere. He went to bed. In order to make it through the night, he took pills, and sometimes he got a full night's sleep without waking up or having nightmares.

He mostly felt like he had an orderly life. That is, orderly for his particular situation—no surprises or unnecessary breakdowns. He didn't do anything, because there was nothing to do; he was no longer anything; he was *no one*. He didn't exist. Given the circumstances, he thought he had managed to do a pretty good job of bringing structure to his life. As he waited for something—he didn't know what.

The social-insurance office was starting to lean on him, and eventually he lost his sick pay. They had to live on

Alexandra's maternity-leave pay and what little of their loans they had left. But it was enough. Alexandra and Nellie spent most of their time at her parents' these days, and he didn't spend much money at all. His mother and Maya filled his cupboards now and then, and once in a while Lia sent Robert over with a bag of foil pans full of leftovers from the school lunch.

One afternoon, Martin takes the car and drives to Adam's day care. He thinks of the day he picked Adam up here for the last time. He saw him that day as a social being, his own person with a life beyond that with his parents. A little taste of the person he would one day be.

Would have been...

The sound of children's voices and laughter seems oddly comforting now, as if a world still exists where no evil can happen. The next day he visits again, but this time he doesn't hear any children outdoors. Maybe they're sleeping right now, or eating? He no longer remembers the schedule.

He is torn from his thoughts by someone knocking on the car window and gesturing for him to roll it down. Only now does he notice the police car parked behind him, next to the day-care fence. A uniformed officer asks to see his driver's license. Martin watches as she reacts to his name.

"You can't loiter here," she says in a friendly tone. "A number of parents have called in. They're worried."

Martin nods. "Okay, I understand. I'm going now."

On the way home he wonders if the parents were just generally anxious because they saw a man in a car outside the day care. Or if they recognized him and knew that, at least statistically, he was a suspect in a crime.

Martin saw his daughter on the days Alexandra was visiting. Never alone. Alexandra would hardly even leave him alone in a room with her. He understood the breadth of how untrustworthy she thought he was, but it didn't bother him. If anything, he agreed. It was as if he had lost the ability to speak up for himself, to have direction in his life, as if he carried no weight anymore. But what was it Alexandra was afraid he would do to Nellie, he wondered? Scare her with the very sight of his face? Drop her? Harm her on purpose?

He couldn't recall the last time he had touched Alexandra, or she him; it was as if he had let everything they'd had go out the window in tiny, shredded bits, without so much as giving it a second thought.

As if he knew that everything that had happened between them had now happened for the last time.

Thoughts sometimes flickered by of what it had been like when they were close. An eternity—or a few months— ago. How he would rub her feet at night, how she would softly whisper "between my toes" or "my heels" or "scratch my little toe" and how he would patiently do as she wished. How she wanted him to tickle that flat spot under the pad of her big toe, just before it met her foot. How he would close his whole hand around her heels and pull his fingers back again and again, like waves. How he would gently scratch the top of her tiny, bowed pinkie toe.

Or how the two of them would curl up together on the sofa when the kids were asleep, how she would settle into the space between his arm and his thigh as they watched a movie, and how one of them always fell asleep.

And he remembered even farther back, how they had lusted after each other when they first lived in the house, when they might stay in bed for an entire weekend. Making love, talking, dozing, playing rock-paper-scissors to see who had to go down to the chilly kitchen and fix some kind of food to bring back upstairs. How he would lie with his head on her belly and whisper loving words to the baby they were expecting, whose heartbeat already seemed to have adapted to the rhythm of the waves.

It almost seemed vulgar when he thought about it now. Such intimacy.

As distant as if it had never happened.

Like a memory that belonged to someone else.

It was edging into spring by the time his life changed again, at least in certain ways.

It started when Maya came for a visit one day when everything frozen outside seemed to be thawing, the rays of spring sunshine slowly loosening winter's chilly grip. The dark brown ground was shedding sheets of ice, and drops of water fell from the roof, bursting brutally against the windowsills.

As they drank their coffee, Maya recounted the final episode of the TV show, which she had watched the night before. She would have to find a new one now, she said, and he nodded in agreement, grateful for the escape from reality she provided for him. True, he couldn't always follow the plot, but her vivid descriptions had a startlingly stimulating effect on him. Then she would sit down and play solitaire as he watched. She made little sounds of displeasure when she turned up the wrong card, and cackled happily when she got a good one.

He followed her movements, her fingers' journey across the shiny surface, the sound of the stiff paper pattering against the table. Her usual muttering.

"There we go."

"Not too bad."

"Oh, what the hell?"

For a moment it seemed like everything was fine. As if life were holy. It had nothing to do with his own personal situation; he understood that was beyond his control. It was more as if reality seemed to be lifted out of its usual context for a brief time, into a dimension where nothing was judged to be this thing or that, or even assigned a value judgment at all.

It was a moment outside the passage of time, where the afternoon sun shone in obliquely across the counter and onto the worn rag rug, as two people sat at a kitchen table and did nothing, or at least not much.

He sometimes wondered how it came to be that she was free during the day. He couldn't recall asking her—about that, or anything else either. Suddenly he felt the urge to do so. Not because he was all that interested in the answer, but because he was curious what it would feel like to ask, to wonder about anything at all. And out of a need to converse, as if he were a regular person just sitting there having coffee with a neighbor who happened to pop by.

"I'm in charge of my own time," she said as her fingers continued to pull cards from the deck.

"Don't you have a husband? Or kids?"

"Nope, not even an ex-husband. Just a cat."

"So what do you do?"

"I'm an artist. A photographer—I have exhibitions sometimes. Right now there's one in Munich and one in Barcelona. Betweentimes I do brief stints as a forensic photographer, with the police. Although since I moved here, I haven't done any of that."

He gazed out the window and went on: "How long have you lived here on Orust?"

Maya squinted, apparently thinking back.

"Since last spring. I live pretty close to Robert and Lia, but I'm sure you knew that. In the eco-village. But I've only traded houses for the time being, with a friend of a friend. I felt like living by the sea, and she wanted a bigger place, preferably in the woods. So we were able to fulfill each other's wishes."

"So she's living in your house?"

"Exactly."

"Where is it?"

"In Dalsland. Outside Åmål. I bought a big old house and fixed it up with a studio, gallery, and living space. And then the forest started to drive me nuts. But it's only temporary—I'm sure I'll go back. Once the sea starts to drive me nuts, if not before."

He raised his eyebrows and felt a twitch at the corner of his mouth, one that could probably be taken for a smile.

"Haven't you done anything here, though? In almost a year?"

"Sure, I've been taking photographs for a new exhibition. About the sea, or at least the surface of it. Mostly by hanging over the edge of a rowboat."

He fixed his eyes on a point of the wall above her head.

"You haven't seen or heard anything weird out there, have you?"

"Weird? Such as?" Maya looked surprised.

He shrugged. "Sounds, maybe? Cries? An old islander Dad knew once said that the fishermen talked about how they sometimes heard cries from the sea in the winter."

Maya laughed, but fell quiet as she met his eyes.

"No," she said simply. "Nothing like that."

He nodded, and silence fell around them once more. It had become their friend; it never felt strained. Not these days, when they were sometimes able to chat and, once in a while, even talk about things that mattered. His clear days were in constant flux with those when he was in a fog, turned away from the world.

"What about you?" she asked at last. "How long have you lived here?"

He was startled. He wasn't prepared to reflect upon himself and his own, discontinued life. She had never asked any personal questions before, but he realized that he had started it.

Maya seemed to notice the transformation in him and adjusted her question.

"I was mostly thinking of the house. How old is it?"

Martin swallowed.

"I think it was built in the late 1800s, as a fisherman's

cottage," he replied. "There was a lot of construction on the island around then."

"Do you know anything about whoever lived here before? Has it been in your family a long time?"

"Mom and Dad bought it in '79, if I remember correctly, before I was born, and it had been empty for a while. They live in Uddevalla but wanted a vacation home out here— my dad is from the island."

"Yes, so Robert said. That must mean you know everything about everyone here on Orust."

"My dad isn't exactly the gossiping type."

He paused.

"I actually have no idea who owned the house before they bought it," he went on. "I suppose I've always meant to find out, but we've been so busy with other things since we moved in, first me and then Alexandra. We had to deal with the most urgent stuff first, heat and drainage, like, fixing the most important things. And then came…"

He fell silent again.

The kids. The words hung unspoken between them.

"And then we had our hands full with that," he said, feeling himself struggling not to fall into the dark abyss. "But there's an attic storage area up in one end of the house, and there's a bunch of boxes there. Left over from people who lived in the house before, including my own parents. I just never got around to going through it."

"Wonderful," said Maya. "It was like that in my attic growing up too. Most of all I remember a whole box full of old magazines from the fifties, mostly pinup ones. I loved to sit up there and page through them."

"I see," Martin said with a faint smile. "I don't know what's up there. Old crap, of course, and some documents. But I think I saw a property abstract up there once, with information about previous owners. And some old maps and blueprints."

Maya shuffled the deck back together and looked him in the eye.

"What are we waiting for?"

Martin hesitated for a moment but then stood up. "Okay, stay here. I'll go get it."

He went up the stairs and over to the low door that led to the storage area. A cold gust of air hit him when he opened it, the dusty smell of decades past.

It had been a long time since anyone had been in here.

He pulled a string, which turned on a light bulb mounted on the ceiling. The faint glow illuminated the cramped space, a few square meters under the sloping roof, full of stacked boxes.

Patiently opening box after box, he ignored the ones that seemed to contain his parents' clothing and belongings, or toys from his own childhood. At the top of one box he found a sketchbook and realized it was his mother's;

he suddenly recalled that she used to draw him while he was playing. At some point she had mentioned that she had spent some time at the Academy of Fine Arts in Copenhagen but had quit when she was forced to admit that she wasn't as talented as she'd thought. He decided to bring the sketchbook down and take a closer look when he had the chance.

He selected two boxes that looked considerably older than the others, and whose top layers consisted of documents and old books, and set them on the landing along with the sketchbook. Then he closed the door again.

His arms were full when he came downstairs, and he caught a flash of curiosity in Maya's eyes. As soon as he opened the first box and found the old, well-thumbed abstract, he gave it to Maya and sat down beside her. She dug her reading glasses out of her purse and carefully began to page through the document. Together they tried to decipher the old-fashioned phrases. They were looking at about a dozen bills of sale and title deeds that had been mounted onto the stiff brown paper of the book; their dates ranged from 1889 until his own parents' purchase in 1979, and the documents seemed to have resisted the passage of time. It appeared that every owner of the house had taken pride in carrying on tradition.

"I love this kind of thing. Talk about your living history,"

Maya said quietly, letting her eyes roam across the elegant writing.

"In 1898 the house was sold to *boatbuilder Mattson* for *five thousand five hundred kronor*," she went on, her index finger slowly tracing the lines.

"And five years later, to *skipper Karl Holmgren* for *seven thousand kronor*," Martin added as she paged ahead.

They sat there for quite a while, becoming absorbed in the handwritten letters that were pressed among the bills of sale and deeds, letters about sons who had traveled to America and mothers who had died in childbirth. Sometimes an incident described in a letter could be linked to the next sale of the house. These were tiny fragments of fates, of the human lives that had been lived within these four walls.

After a while, Maya's phone dinged.

"Unfortunately I'm going to have to come back to this another day," she said as she read the message. "The plumber is on his way. He's hard to pin down, and I have to take the chance while I've got it, so I can get my dripping faucet fixed. It's keeping me awake at night."

Once she had left, Martin sat quietly for a while, staring at nothing. As if Maya had been the engine of all of this, a driving force that was now gone.

He took out his mother's sketchbook and paged through

it. Most of the drawings, which were in pencil or marker, appeared to be just for practice: perspective sketches of buildings and furniture, body parts, vases, flowers. Others were landscapes, many with motifs from the sea. Some showed Martin as a little boy. His father was there in a few of them; they wandered hand in hand along the beach or kicked a ball in the yard. One depicted the two of them sitting at the kitchen table in Uddevalla with a Lego tower in front of them. Strange, he couldn't remember Dad ever doing stuff like this with him. He felt an unexpected surge of tenderness.

He turned the page. The next sketch was so violently crossed out, as if in a rage, that at first he couldn't tell what it was. When he turned it over and studied it from the back, he was able to make out the subject. It seemed to be the rocky beach below the house in Ekevik. On the big rock stood a small figure, leaning forward, fully dressed, both arms out to the sides. Like a cross, like he was just about to jump in—or fall. He had a vague memory of his mother rescuing him one time when he fell into the water. Was that the scene depicted in this sketch? Why had she tried to hide it?

He put the pad aside and tackled the second box.

It was a little bigger and heavier.

When he first opened it, he wasn't sure what he was looking at, just that it was something…terrible, something tremendous, something that threatened him to his very core.

He saw two numbers glaring up at him, like razor-sharp teeth in the maw of an evil monster.

A one and a one, together.

11.

And then *January.*

11 January.

It was one of those old calendars where you tore off one page per day.

And it *was* old—from 1965. Someone had stashed it here among a lot of other papers. That date was at the very top, and it wouldn't have been remarkable at all if it weren't for the date itself, those ones, and at first he couldn't understand why; he hardly even knew he remembered.

Remembered what?

The date.

That was right; that was it.

January 11 was the day Adam had disappeared.

The road that led down to the brothers' house must have been paved once upon a time, but now Maya guessed the asphalt had been worn away by heavy vehicles and machinery. She found that she would have to drive straight through the farmyard to reach the spot by the water where Martin kept his gear.

Good, she thought. She wanted to have a look around.

On one side of the yard was a long barn; on the other was a garage full of farm implements. Just to the right of the road, a short way in, was the house, a big ramshackle hulk with a patched tin roof and outbuildings in every direction. It looked as if the brothers were barely keeping the whole thing from collapsing.

In front of the house were a few old cars, a moped, and several bicycles. She saw the flickering blue light of a TV coming from one of the ground-floor windows. Otherwise everything seemed quiet.

She kept going down toward the water. Now she could see

the small beach, the dock, and the boathouse, with a fresh coat of the traditional red paint. She parked and stepped out.

When she saw the spot, she once again understood, a little, why the brothers might have been annoyed with Martin after he got permission from the municipality to run his mussel farm and keep his gear there.

Sure, Martin had the law on his side, but still.

She could imagine how the brothers and their family had considered the spot their own over the years, swimming there in the summer and skating in the winter; maybe they'd kept a boat of their own for fishing trips. If she understood correctly, they had even been able to use the boathouse to store their grill and fishing gear.

Now there was room only for Martin's stuff.

Would that be reason enough to sabotage the mussel farm? Sure, why not?

But if that didn't have the intended effect, would it be reason enough to kidnap the mussel farmer's little boy? Causing Martin to be so done in by grief as to take the mussel farm with him? Who could say? But was it really likely that the brothers would be so cruel? Would they dare to take such serious risks? They must have known that after all the threats they'd made, they would be suspects. Or were they not that smart? What was the deal with inbreeding on islands? she wondered, full of prejudice. That was only in the olden days, right?

Her eyes wandered across Martin's gear as she distract-edly made mental notes.

Tied up at the dock was a large rowboat with some sort of crane on one end. On land lay about two dozen plastic buoys, which looked like stacked barrels, and inside the boathouse she could see piles of nets and big bags of farming ropes.

She wanted to give herself time. Create a reason to come back again and again. Today she would just find out how much gear they were talking about here, what kind of equipment she would need to remove it, and how many times she would have to drive over. And she would initiate contact with the brothers. Or *try* to.

She began to walk up the hill. After a while she could see the back of the house and the overgrown garden.

She walked around the house and knocked on the front door. It was a brief and cautious knock, just for appearances' sake; it was hardly even audible. Then she strolled down the driveway a bit, slightly distracted, casting hasty glances at the cars, a rusty Toyota and a beat-up Volvo.

Then she returned to the back of the house. She peered into a basement window on the way. Laundry room. Work-bench. Some kind of storage area, crammed full.

One window was boarded up from the inside. It looked like it had been done with care, not just as a random way to keep anyone from looking in. And the boards looked brand new: clean and white.

She found the cellar door and knocked there.

No response.

She tested the handle. The door was open.

"Who are you?"

He had come up right beside her, so close she could smell his sour breath. The grass had muffled his steps.

Maya jumped, startled, and closed the door.

"I'm sorry," she said. "I knocked but no one answered. I tried the front door too."

The man was wearing baggy blue coveralls with stains left by oil and paint. He had a stubbly beard that lay like a sparse coat of fur across his sunken cheeks and his chin.

"Oho. Is that so?"

He was holding a tool, something like a clamp, in his large, grubby hands. His fingers spun a loose part of it around and around.

"The thing is…" Maya began, feeling vaguely threatened. He was standing way too close. "I'm a good friend of Martin's, and I'm here to help him collect the gear down by the water."

He watched her suspiciously.

"Is that so?"

"Yes." She took a cautious step back.

"Well, that's good to hear," he said, without taking his

eyes from her. "We've been…wondering about that, you might say. What the hell it's doing there, and so forth."

"I get it," Maya said. "Kind of weird. That he got permission to be there, I mean."

"Well, it was the municipality that made sure of that. I guess it made no difference to them that our family had been using that spot for probably a hundred years. Pretty damn lazy of them, if you ask me. But that's the way it is. Everything has to be so modern these days, and mussel farms are so trendy now, they want to support them. It must bring in major moolah for the government."

Maya gave a stiff smile.

"Anyway, it's all going to be cleared out now," she said. "No more mussel farm."

"Really?" It looked like he was trying to hide his enthusiasm, but his voice gave him away. "So it didn't work out, then, the farm?"

"I don't know all the details, but I heard he had some problems with sabotage. With the anchor lines. A while ago."

"I'm sure it was just those dang Jet Skis. They drive like maniacs, those guys. That crap shouldn't be allowed, if you ask me."

"But now he's… Well, you've heard, right? About his boy?"

The man nodded slowly. As if the more slowly he nodded, the more sympathy he was showing.

"Yeah, I heard about that. It was…"

He ran an oily fingertip across his cheek.

"Aw, damn. Four years old, is that right?"

"Three and a bit."

"Damn. You've barely learned to swim by that age. Got to keep an eye on the little ones."

"Yeah," said Maya.

"Okay, well, now I know."

"Anyway, I just wanted to show my face so you know who I am when I'm around. I just came over to check it out this time, how much stuff there is and so on. I'll be back later on with a trailer," said Maya.

"Oh. So it'll be a while?"

"Not too long."

"Okay, but see to it that it happens. We've been patient long enough about all that crap."

No one said anything for a moment.

"Just one last thing…" Maya said at last. "Could I maybe borrow your bathroom? It's kind of an emergency."

The man looked at her. Maya couldn't interpret his expression, couldn't tell if he thought she was crossing a line.

"Sure," he said after a moment. "Follow me."

They walked around the house. The odor of fried pork and coffee struck her as he opened the front door. The sound of what she guessed was a video game blended with the chatter of a radio station.

"What's the deal with all of that, by the way?" the man said, his back to her. "Are they sure the boy drowned?"

Maya waited for him to turn toward her before responding. His gaze darted around, as if he didn't dare make eye contact with her.

"No," she said. "They can't be sure until they find the body and can determine what happened to it."

"Right. So what do they think…might have happened otherwise?"

"Well…" Maya said, letting her voice trail off. "He could have disappeared some other way, gotten lost, frozen to death. He might be lying in a barn somewhere."

The man nodded stoically.

"But they did search for him nearby, so maybe that's not very likely. Were they here?" she went on.

"Who?"

"The police and the civil patrol. Missing People."

He nodded. "Oh, right. Yes, they searched everything."

"The house too?"

"Of course. Or maybe not the house. But everything else."

"It could be that someone took him and is hiding him somewhere," Maya said. "That will make it a lot harder. And more serious."

"But the police sure seemed to give up quickly. If they truly suspected something, I'm sure they would have turned the whole damn island upside down."

"Sure, but who knows what the investigation will find. The case is still open," Maya pointed out.

"There's the bathroom," he said, pointing at a door right beside them.

"Thanks," Maya said.

She turned to him.

"My name's Maya, by the way," she said, putting out her hand.

"Robin. And that's my brother, Jonatan." He gestured toward the living room.

Maya peered in and saw a guy in a swivel chair with a video-game controller in his hands. In a room past that one, a woman was curled up on a sofa, apparently absorbed in a magazine.

"Hi," Maya said, raising a hand.

The brother gave her a cursory glance and nod before turning back to the TV.

The bathroom was cramped and dirty. A pile of car magazines lay on the floor beneath the sink.

Maya pretended to relieve herself, then flushed the toilet and turned on the faucet. While the water was running, she cautiously opened the chipped cabinet, which didn't contain much: painkillers, toothbrushes, shaving items, an ointment or two. Her eyes were drawn to a bag from the pharmacy, and her heart began to pound as she saw what was inside: a colorful box with Bamse the bear on it. Children's bandages!

As soon as she closed the bathroom door behind her on her way out, she wished she had snapped a photo of the box on her phone. As evidence.

Robin was gone. Jonatan kept playing without so much as a glance her way. The woman was nowhere in sight.

Before Maya left, she looked at the door she assumed led into the basement.

Someone had recently boarded over a window down there, and she had to know why.

She would get down there somehow. She recognized this excitement from the times she had collaborated with the police; she was like a dog on a scent trail.

Instead of just calling, Maya decided to visit the police station to ask about the threatening letters. She went there one morning, since she knew from experience it wouldn't be as busy then. A young, friendly officer who said her name was Anna took the time to listen to Maya once she'd explained her background as a forensic photographer.

Anna confirmed that they still had both letters—the one Mattias at the diving club had told her about and the one Martin had handed over. They weren't close at hand, but she showed Maya an archived photo of the diving club's letter on the computer. Apparently the fact that Maya had mentioned the NYPD had made an impression and prompted Anna to bend the rules a little. Maya immediately recognized both the marker writing and the pale blue envelope.

"But we've had no reason to investigate these cases further," Anna said.

"And no more threatening letters have been brought in?"

Anna laughed.

"Sure, tons of them. We have a few citizens in this district who send more or less threatening letters to anyone who gets on their bad side. To cat owners who allow their darling pets to use their sandboxes as a bathroom, to neighbors whose trees are blocking their sunlight, or to women who sunbathe topless on the beach in plain sight. You name it. We archive all the letters we get in, but hardly anything ever really happens. Whether any of them looked exactly like this one, I really can't say."

Next Maya asked whether anything had turned up in the case of Adam's disappearance, but Anna would confirm only that the case was still open, even though it was assumed that the boy had drowned.

"So nothing new has come up? No tips from the public?"

"No, nothing useful."

"What do you mean by 'useful'?"

"In a missing-persons case, there are always lots of people who contact us, sure that they've seen the victim here or there. Yesterday a lady called to tell us that Adam had been taken by the same person who kidnapped little Madeleine in Portugal years ago. She insisted she had seen the two of them together on a street in Bangkok."

"Have you had any other recent cases around here with kids going missing?"

"No, like I said, it's unusual. Of course, there have been a couple of tragic but confirmed drownings in the past decade. Unfortunately that's just reality on an island. And a few children have gotten lost in the woods, but we usually find them pretty quickly."

"What about children who have been assaulted or sexually abused?"

"That happens all over, of course."

Anna suddenly looked grim and stood up abruptly, signaling that this meeting was over.

⌒

He brought his index and middle fingers together, gently resting them on her forehead and running them down along her nose, across her lips, chin, and throat, and on under the covers and between her breasts, until they landed in her navel.

Bäcke lay on his side in the bed, his massive body casting a shadow over her own. Maya laughed suddenly.

"What's so funny?"

"It just occurred to me that I look like a lake flowing outward in all directions, and you look like a mountain."

He propped his head up in his palm.

"Are you flowing out in all directions?"

"Toned muscles have never been my thing, as you may have noticed. And I like good food."

He hummed in response and continued to run his fingers down her body.

"Listen..." he said softly.

"What?"

"What do you *do* over at that guy Martin's place?"

She had been expecting the question.

"Are you jealous?"

He didn't reply right away.

"A little," he said at last.

She sighed.

"Well, you can't be if you're going to be with me."

Her tone was friendly, but it contained a level of confidence that left no doubt she was serious.

"Or to be more specific, you can't let it get the better of you. It would make your life miserable."

He gazed at her, his face so close that she could see every strand of hair, every pore on his face.

"I have to be free to live my life," she went on, lowering her voice to a whisper. "But I'm not sleeping with anyone else at the moment. I can promise you that. And I'll have you know that it's not often I can promise that sort of thing."

He almost jumped.

"It isn't?"

"Not exactly."

He turned onto his back, letting out a sigh that turned into a laugh of some sort.

"Okay then."

"I hope the feeling is mutual," she said.

"I'm an old man," he said. "I wouldn't have the energy to keep more than one relationship going at once, even if I wanted to."

"Well, would you want to?"

"No, I'm hopelessly monogamous by my very nature and out of habit." He looked at her again. "Can't I still ask, though? What you do at his place? If I promise that I...won't express any jealousy?"

Maya smiled.

"We don't talk much. We mostly just sit together. Playing cards, doing crosswords, stuff like that. And I like to tell him about TV shows, to get him...how should I put it...to be *present*. He's apt to get lost in his own mind, in his own guilt. He's a broken man, and I think for some reason he appreciates my company. Maybe because I'm a stranger to him, and I can't ask anything of him or demand any explanations."

"But what do you get out of it? You're hardly the self-sacrificing type."

"I'm just following an impulse. I'm not sure I can explain it."

"Try."

She stared straight ahead.

"Besides the fact that I'm interested in what might have happened to the boy, there's something about…the passivity of it all…That's what I was drawn to at first."

"What do you mean?"

"His passivity. In some sense I found it relaxing to be with someone who had gotten off the train."

"The train?"

"Of life. His whole life."

He rubbed his hand over his face.

"I don't get it," he said. "It doesn't sound healthy. It's tragic—that's all there is to it. He has another kid."

"I don't really get it either. But then…one day, he started talking about the sea and his diving, and he became a different Martin. So engaged and full of life, even attractive. Until that point, I had only seen him as a victim. You know, I was so moved that I even thought about learning to dive so I could retrain myself into an underwater photographer."

He rolled his eyes.

"I hope that urge has passed."

"I'm not so sure. We'll see. And anyway, Robert was the one who originally asked if I could keep an eye on how Martin was doing. He was worried about him."

She realized that they were standing at a crossroads, perhaps their first major one. Would his inability to understand her behavior and her way of looking at relationships cause him to start distancing himself, or would he simply accept that he didn't understand, and move on?

He got out of bed, pulled on his robe, and went to the kitchen. She stayed put, feeling uncertain. A little scared that he would turn away from her. Maybe she shouldn't have gone so hard with her insistence on being the person she was. On being free. Maybe she would have to learn to compromise.

She turned onto her stomach and buried her face in the pillow. The worry was spreading through her chest; she wasn't used to feeling this way. Had she ever even been afraid of losing someone before?

She'd always imagined that if she ever truly fell for a man, he would be a very complex person, multifaceted, intellectual, maybe downright reserved. A man she constantly had to challenge, and who challenged her in return. Bäcke wasn't like that at all. He was uncomplicated; he was kindness and stability personified.

Wouldn't she get tired of that after a while? Get bored?

She tried to listen for activity in the kitchen, hear what he was doing. The radio came on. A scent. Coffee?

After a while he came back to the bedroom. He sat down and bent over her, kissing her lips.

"Breakfast is served, my pearl."

The fragile acceptance Alexandra had managed to nurture in herself when it came to Adam's death had crumbled after her visit to the healer. It now felt more impossible than ever for her to take on Martin's problems as well, so she decided to stay with her parents for a while longer. Her childhood room, which hadn't been changed since she moved out at the age of twenty, felt more like a home than the silent cottage in Ekevik.

She changed Nellie's diaper, dressed her, and stuck her into the stroller to go shopping at the nearby grocery store. She was standing in one of the aisles when a lady came up to her and spoke to her in a whisper.

"Aren't you Alexandra, little Adam's mother?"

Alexandra gave a curt nod. She didn't speak to journalists, nor, for that matter, to people who walked right up to express their sympathy. Such moments always brought her to the brink of tears.

"I've tried to call so many times," the woman whispered. "But neither you nor the boy's father ever pick up."

"No, that's true. A lot of people have been calling. What is this all about?"

"What luck that I caught you. I followed you here from your parents' place." The woman looked around anxiously and went on: "We can't talk here. Can we meet somewhere else?"

"No, I don't think…"

"There's a café called Fikastunden on the next cross street over. I'll be there at three, both today and tomorrow."

The woman disappeared to some other part of the store, and Alexandra resumed shopping. She felt like she had landed in a bad spy movie, with whispered encounters in the diaper aisle.

When she had finished her last errand and was about to head home, she realized she would be passing the café the woman had mentioned. It was quarter to three, so maybe she should treat herself to a cup of tea and a sandwich and hear what the woman was after. *What if…what if!* She couldn't afford to miss out on even the most unlikely chance for a clue.

The woman was already there when Alexandra battled her way to the back with the big stroller. She ordered and took a seat at the woman's table.

"I think he's got him," the woman said, with no prelude.

She was still whispering and never took her eye off the door.

Alexandra studied the pieces of a shredded napkin that were strewn across the red-checked tablecloth like confetti. She saw the woman's trembling hands, her bitten nails.

"Someone has my son? Is that what you mean? What's your name, by the way?"

"Annette. It's my neighbor, Bo. Bosse. I've seen the little boy a number of times over the past few months, in the yard. I recognize him from the newspapers, his blue jacket too. He's middle-aged. No kids. No family. And an oddball sort, that one, always staring at you creepily. There are rumors that he spent time in prison."

"Have you talked to the police?"

"No…I'm scared to. As a single woman…I'm sure he'd get violent if he found out that…" She talked fast, in staccato.

"Thanks for the tip," Alexandra said, and stood up without waiting for her tea. "If you give me his name and address, I'll look into it." She didn't believe this woman for a moment, but she could still inform the police.

The address Annette had given her wasn't far from her parents' apartment, and after dinner that same day she decided to take an evening walk and go by. The house was in bad shape, and the yard was completely overgrown. She peered through a hole in the tall fence and saw something that looked like rabbit cages behind the house. A TV was on upstairs. Sure enough, she could see that the next house over, which she guessed was Annette's, would provide a view straight into the yard. On the following evenings, too, Alexandra walked by but never saw anything to suggest a child was there. A few times she saw the man who lived in the house; he moved slowly and his back was stooped, and he didn't make a particularly scary impression.

To be on the safe side, Alexandra called the police, who only sighed when she told them about Annette and her observations.

"That woman has been at odds with her neighbor for as long as I've worked at this station. I don't know what he did to her. You'd never believe me if I told you the terrible things she's reported him for over the years. We've looked into him, of course, and all we found was a parking ticket from 2009. He's not what you'd call social, but in all likelihood he is perfectly harmless. And probably a much better person than she is."

"Are you saying that she's a tinfoil hatter?"

"Your words, not mine," said the police officer. "Basically, but if you want me to, I'll make sure some patrol cars take that road to keep an eye on that house now and then."

Alexandra thanked them for the help; she had never pinned great hopes on that woman's whispers.

3

Was it a coincidence? Or a bad omen, a malevolent sign? He looked at the old calendar. The cardboard had yellowed from the corners in, like a tide slowly drawing ashore a little bit each year.

The calendar was full of empty squares where you were supposed to stick a picture for every month. January's picture was there: a hare in its winter coat, bounding between trees. The other stickers were still on a small pad above the date pages.

The dates, right. Someone had torn away pages until January 11, 1965. After that, no more pages had been removed.

It was as if time had stopped in this house on January 11, 1965, almost fifty-five years ago, just as it had stopped on January 11 of this year.

The deed book.

He grabbed it and quickly paged to near the end.

An Arvid Svensson had bought the house on March 1, 1962.

Three years later, in the spring of 1965, Arvid Svensson's estate had sold the house to an Olof Melander.

Martin searched on through the box. It looked like someone had taken things off tables and walls and placed them there: embroidered wall hangings, a few photographs, paintings and table runners. A couple of the photographs were family portraits. Martin guessed that Arvid Svensson was the stylish young man in a suit with slicked-down hair in almost every image and that the woman in fashionable patterned dresses with beehive hairdos was his wife. In a few of the color photos was a child, a girl. At her oldest, she looked about eight.

Lively, mischievous eyes. Lots of energy—she couldn't sit still for long, Martin imagined.

Would a new homeowner one day in the future find a box like this in the attic full of his and Alexandra's lives? And Adam's? The green-striped boot that had washed up from the sea, the rocks he had collected, Mulle the doll, the little blue-and-yellow plastic boat he always played with in the bath as they sang "Row, Row, Row Your Boat"?

Along one edge of the box was a newspaper. It was the local *Bohusläningen*, from January 12, 1965.

Martin unfolded the large paper.

The whole front page was dominated by one story, with a bold headline and one of the family pictures Martin had just seen in the box.

FAMILY FALLS THROUGH ICE

Sunday outing ends in tragedy. Two adults and a child drowned yesterday near Nösund on Orust. They fell through the ice on their way home from an outing to a nearby islet. Only the daughter's friend, who had accompanied them, survived.

On Sunday, dentist Arvid Svensson and his wife, Marianne, a schoolteacher, took their eight-year-old daughter, Lena, and her friend on an ice-skating trip across the bay near their home.

In recent years, thin ice has become the norm around the islands of Bohuslän, but this year the ice has been thick for several weeks. Apparently, however, there were weak spots in this location at this particular time, and other skaters in the vicinity witnessed these persons falling in one by one as they tried to help one another.

By the time the first onlookers arrived to render aid, the daughter's friend was the only one who hadn't fallen in. The other skaters helped the girl make her way to safety on land, where she could be attended to by rescue workers.

Next of kin have been notified and have approved the publication of this notice, as they hope, in doing so, to inspire others to be cautious and avoid a similar fate.

Martin could hardly breathe as he read.

Murky darkness had settled over the room, so he turned on the light over the table, realizing he was full of an eagerness he didn't recognize, couldn't remember having had for a long time.

Three people drowned in the same water, in the same place, and on the same date as his Adam had disappeared, more than half a century earlier.

What did it mean?

Maybe nothing, but it was remarkable to say the least.

He leaned back and tried to relax, wondering if he truly had never heard this story before, imagining that the memories might come easier if he let his mind wander freely. This had all happened years before he was born, true, but these people had lived in his same house, and there seemed to have been only one owner between them and his parents.

They'd never mentioned it, as far as he could recall.

He had to ask them. They weren't the type to discuss anything beyond what was necessary, so maybe it was down to that.

Why dwell on such terrible things? What good could it possibly do?

He could hear his mother's voice. The very thought annoyed him; he knew this would be her response if he asked.

Martin stood up, went to the pantry, and took out a can of ravioli. He opened it with the wall-mounted can opener, took a fork from the silverware drawer, and began to eat.

It tasted like metal and sour tomatoes.

He put down the can, went back to the box, and found a faded photograph of the little girl.

Lena.

Slightly upturned nose; freckles; thin, pale lips. Long, thick hair.

Without thinking about what he was doing, he went to get the thumbtacks from a drawer in the kitchen. Then he went to the sunroom, where a preschool portrait of Adam hung on the wall.

He took out one tack and stuck the photo onto the wallpaper beside Adam's.

Lena. Adam.

Now Adam wasn't alone anymore, there in the depths.

Bäcke invited Maya to Saturday dinner the next week. Unlike her, he was as skilled in the kitchen as he was enthusiastic about cooking, and she often ate at his place.

"Is it a special occasion, if you're inviting me so far ahead of time?" she wondered. "You're usually so spontaneous about our meals. Will other people be coming too?"

"It so happens it's my birthday," he said. "And I thought it might be a good chance for you to get to know my son and his girlfriend."

Maya was nonplussed. She didn't want to get too involved with his family. She would be moving back to Dalsland soon enough, and she'd imagined their farewell to be the simplest possible kind. No scenes, no excessive feelings. That was how she wanted it. Right?

But she couldn't exactly turn down his birthday dinner.

On Saturday evening, Maya put some thought into how she dressed, for once. A low-cut flowery dress, shoes with a small heel, a touch of mascara, and to top it all off, bright red lipstick.

"Pretty, but not gaudy," she muttered to her reflection in the mirror.

She called a cab; if Jocke and his girlfriend were sleeping at Bäcke's, she wasn't going to stay over. And she certainly intended to have wine with dinner on a night like this. It was silly, but she felt nervous.

Bäcke was delighted by the books about sculpture she had bought for him. He was wearing a freshly ironed white cotton shirt and a pair of gray chinos, and she had never seen him looking so tidy. Embarrassingly enough, she didn't even know what birthday this was—she'd never asked his age, and it didn't seem like the right moment now.

Jocke was around twenty-five and wore his blond hair in a little knot atop his head. He had a bushy Viking beard. His girlfriend, Annika, was small and trim, and her child-like face with its big blue eyes made her look like a pixie. Was she even an adult yet? Maya wondered.

To Maya's surprise, it turned out to be a very pleasant evening. Bäcke had made a vegan dish with corn on the cob, coconut milk, and lime, and for dessert they had a vegan lemon cheesecake with raspberries. And there was even after-dinner coffee; for some reason Maya had gotten the idea that vegans couldn't have coffee—it was too delicious—but apparently they weren't that deprived.

As they drank their coffee, Jocke stood up to deliver a birthday speech and lead a cheer for Bäcke.

"And now," he concluded, "Annika and I have a little surprise for you. You're going to be a grandpa, Dad. Annika and I are going to have a baby."

Bäcke's surprise and his joy almost made Maya's heart hurt. But did she really want to be part of this? Did she even want to know this? *Her*, a step-grandma?

Maya and Annika cleaned up together as Bäcke took Jocke out to the yard to show him the sculpture he was working on.

"How did you two meet?" Maya asked, in want of other, more original topics of conversation. She felt that she ought to show some engagement, for Bäcke's sake.

"It was last fall, at a protest against a company that was releasing all this plastic into the sea."

"Do you both live in the collective?"

"Yes, we have for a while, but now we're thinking of getting our own place. A collective isn't ideal when you have little kids."

"Where do you work?" Maya wondered as she loaded the dishwasher.

"I'm a marine biologist."

"Whoa, and here I thought you looked so terribly young."

Annika smiled cheerfully. "I'm twenty-seven."

Maya was ashamed of her hasty judgment, and not for the first time.

When the kitchen was straightened, she thanked everyone for the evening and, full of mixed feelings, got in the taxi for the ride home. She had felt her roots digging just a little deeper into the Orust soil this evening. She had to be careful.

The sun had begun its arc across the bright blue sky and was spreading its rays across the landscape.

Maya had a front-row seat at her own computer as she drank her morning coffee and worked on her latest water photographs; she'd gone out alone in the middle of the night and come home at three to sleep for six hours. Bäcke had stayed home this time. He needed to get to work early because he was temping as an assistant at a home for the mentally ill.

Instead of using Bäcke to anchor herself, she had latched herself to the boat and placed a bag of weights in the back.

The photographs had turned out unexpectedly good. The dark sky had reflected off the water and made the surface structure almost invisible to the eye—yet the details were there, and in sharp focus, for there had been a clear, starry sky. She was pleased.

Lia came over out of the blue for coffee and a chat. She'd brought a huge bouquet of flowers.

"Oh, those are beautiful. Are they for me?" Maya asked in surprise. "It's not my birthday or anything."

"I know, but I need to get rid of them somehow. Robert helped his mother at the florist's yesterday, and she always sends a ton of flowers home with him, stuff that never lasts long. It'd be nice if she gave him some payment instead. Anyway, it gives me such a headache—the whole house smells like a funeral."

Lia told Maya she was trying to recruit some friends to start a book club. Was Maya interested?

"But I'm not going to be here for very long."

"I know, and I'll miss you a lot—Agneta's so terrifyingly fastidious—but you can just participate for as long as you're here. It won't be very official. We'll have a good dinner together, drink a glass of wine, shoot the shit, and wind up by chatting about the book. Just hanging out."

"Okay, cool, maybe we can get Alexandra to join. She's a professional, after all—who could be a better advisor than a librarian? She must be starting back at work again soon, and she could probably use a distraction."

It was decided that Maya would talk to Alexandra when she got the chance.

That afternoon, Maya was on her way to Martin's. Just as she was about to pass the driveway to Robin and

Jonatan's farm, they went by in the opposite direction. They had turned onto the rural road right before her eyes.

Robin was driving; Jonatan was reclining in the passenger seat and drinking from a big soda bottle. They didn't seem to notice her.

She passed the driveway and veered into a parking spot until they were out of sight. Then she turned back and drove into their yard.

She had no idea how long they would be gone, but she just couldn't resist such an opportunity now that it had presented itself.

A variety of excuses swirled in the back of her mind, things she could say if they discovered her. None of them sounded promising.

She would have to improvise if needed.

Driving past the farmyard, she parked halfway down to the water. This way the car wouldn't be visible from the house but would still be close enough to it for her to walk there. She crept up to the house.

Someone had put a wheelbarrow in front of the little basement window that was boarded up from the inside. Over it lay a tarp that obscured the whole window. Hardly a coincidence, Maya thought, lifting the tarp.

The wheelbarrow was full of gravel.

She walked up to the yard and made a circuit around the

car that was still in the driveway. Then she went back to check the cellar door. Locked.

Next she went to the front of the house, stepped onto the stoop, knocked, and tried the door handle. All was quiet in the house, and that door was locked as well.

She looked around. No one could see her. No one could be sitting in a nearby kitchen window and watching her, wondering what she was doing there. Which was lucky, since there could be no denying that her actions would seem rather baffling, if not downright suspicious.

Imagining that all homeowners kept an extra set of keys somewhere outside the house, she began to search. She looked under the flowerpot that held what looked like a wilted fern. She searched through the damp banana crates full of newspapers and trash, and under the medium-sized rocks on either side of the stoop.

Just as she was about to give up, she glanced at the doormat. It was heavy and thick and could probably hide just about anything.

Could it be that simple?

Well, damn!

There it was. *It must be a mistake*, Maya thought. *Someone must have put it there a long time ago and then forgotten about it.* It seemed absurd. But maybe there was nothing in the house worth stealing.

She could still turn back. It wasn't too late. She hadn't done anything yet.

But she was about to cross a line. Never before had she done something like this. Sure, she'd wormed her way into other people's houses in lots of different circumstances, but always by talking her way in, although she did sometimes stretch the truth.

Screw it, she thought.

And she unlocked the door and went in.

As she stood in the brothers' hall, she was extremely aware that there would be no way to defend her actions now. She tried to call up an image of Adam to assuage her guilty conscience, but it didn't work.

She could be reported to the authorities. Punished. She might never be able to work with the police again. And what would happen if one of those creepy brothers caught her red-handed?

Standing in a quiet, strange house like this, it was as if the silence itself were pointing fingers at her. As if everything around her were glaring at her: the big, empty shoes, the heavy jackets hanging in the hall, the discolored wallpaper, a pair of mass-produced paintings in flimsy frames. The dim rooms, the kitchen in one direction and the living room in the other, the stairs straight ahead.

She made a snap decision and locked the front door

from the inside. Then she went over to what she guessed was the basement door and opened it.

A cold, damp gust hit her, like an underground breeze, an ominous breath.

The staircase was narrow and steep, and it turned to the right. Its walls were clad in rough brown planks. If you were to run your palm over them, you would end up with hundreds of splinters; it would take hours to pick them out.

She wondered how many times the brothers had failed to resist the temptation.

Each step revealed her presence, the protracted creaks leading her farther and farther into the chilly darkness. It felt so far away. So many squeaks, so many sounds.

At last she reached the bottom. The chill bit into her as if it were setting its teeth, gnawing its way in.

She climbed over piles of dirty laundry, an old still, a couple of big engines, and a bunch of boxes as she made her way to the cellar door that led out. The key was in the lock, and the light streamed in when she unlocked and opened the door. Her heart skittering like a frightened creature, she went out and back around the house, where she replaced the key under the doormat on the stoop, then returned to the basement and locked the door behind her.

Now she would have plenty of time if they returned home; they'd have no reason to suspect anything was up.

They would find the doors locked just as they had been when the brothers left the house.

She tried to get her bearings. Here and there, pale daylight made it through the small, dirty windows. She didn't want to turn on any lights.

There were three doors to choose from. Two of them were ajar; inside were what looked to be a laundry room and a workshop, respectively—the rooms she had seen from outside last time.

The third door was locked, but the key was in it.

She opened it.

The room was pitch black.

She looked for a light switch, found it outside the door, and brought a flickering fluorescent tube to life.

The first thing that came to her mind was *I was right*. But her triumph was soon dampened by the grim reality of what it might mean.

It was a small room, almost entirely devoid of objects.

Except for the foam squares on the walls. Soundproofing.

Except for a mattress on the floor.

And except for what was on the mattress: a blanket. And a teddy bear.

At that moment, she heard a car coming up the gravel driveway.

For the first time in ages, Martin got out of bed before the old grandfather clock downstairs struck eleven in the morning. It had served as a benchmark of sorts throughout the passing days; he had counted its strokes, let them sound up through the floor, through him.

It seemed to him these days that time took up so little space in a physical sense. A tiny corner of everyone's phone screen. In this house, time was allowed to expand, force him out if it wanted to; time could tick and hum and strike unrestrained. Twenty-four hours a day, it was allowed to take up a decent chunk of the wall, from floor to ceiling, with its hand-painted blue-pine casing.

Adam and I used to . . .

It slashed through him. Really *slashed*.

They used to count the strokes from downstairs at Adam's bedtime. They seldom made it past eight. Adam had only been three and hadn't been allowed to stay up any later.

Nine, maybe, once in a while, and it was always cause for excitement. Nine strokes!

Can I stay up until a thousand someday, Papa?

He headed straight for the shower—this was remarkable too. Turning on the hot water, he let it envelop him, lathering himself with the last sliver of soap and squeezing one empty shampoo bottle after the next until he found some specialty shampoo for henna-treated hair that Alexandra's sister had left behind one time.

Hair's hair, he thought.

He found the beard trimmer, adjusted it, and ran it over his thick, tangled beard until the trimmer screeched in protest. No dice—instead he shaved off his beard entirely. He thought about shaving his head as well—didn't monks do that as a sign of penitence? But he refrained.

His mother must have washed his clothes and put them away in his dresser, because he found both jeans and T-shirts there. He realized that he should thank her, that he should have done so many times by now, but it all took too much energy; it was too difficult, too demanding. Each word was like a weight he had to struggle to pull out of himself, out of the darkness. Maya was the only one he could sometimes talk to. She came and went, but she never stirred up any feelings inside him.

He ate two bananas and drank a big cup of coffee.

Then he went out.

He stood on the steps for a while, letting his eyes rove over the yard. The afternoon rain hung in the sky like floating humidity—dense but weightless little drops that didn't want to fall, as if the sea were clinging to the nothingness.

The trees and bushes were green, a fresh green, still not yellowed. Spring, he thought, but then he realized he wasn't sure whether this was the same year Adam had disappeared, or if a whole year had already passed. Had it been summer yet? Christmas? Had a Christmas passed, without Adam? Was his fourth birthday over? He got in the car. Turned the key.

The car started.

It felt like a miracle. Or maybe it wasn't. He didn't know when he'd last driven it; maybe it wasn't so long ago.

He plugged his phone into the charger and saw the screen light up. After a moment, the date appeared.

May 4, 2019.

Maybe he wasn't so bad off after all. He sat up straight. He was on the right path. He had no idea what the path was or where it led, but something inside him seemed to ignite; something was going his way, pointing in a different direction, in the right direction, if only for today.

Not once had he left the property since Adam vanished. Although…no, could that really be true? He searched his memory but couldn't think of when he might have left. Had he gone to the day care? These roads were like a distant memory. As though he were a veteran of war returning after years to a now-strange country.

He simply drifted around without a goal in mind, hunched over the wheel, his eyes roaming all the pale green that spread out before him, around him. The rural road was like a dead snake, electrical wires and masts crisscrossing the sky, speed cameras watching, signs pointing this way and that.

RECYCLING CENTER. DISCOUNT STORE. SWIMMING BEACH. HISTORICAL MONUMENT.

He drove in circles for a few hours, many kilometers back and forth but never very far from home. He just wanted to reconquer his territory. The country store, the day care, Henån and all its stores. The eco-village, Slussen.

His life.

Did he want to go back?

At last he realized he was on his way to Mollösund.

The road wound its way through a valley that, like large portions of the island, had once been at the bottom of the sea. Steep hills rose all around. As he approached the town, he saw the wind whipping up whitecaps on the sea.

All that lay between the old fishing village and the open water was the neighboring island of Mollön, which was nestled between them like a protective levee.

He passed the cemetery, where a fifth of the population had been buried when cholera ravaged the town in the 1800s. Then he parked outside the inn and looked at the time.

Two thirty. Perhaps too late for lunch. He hoped it was Sven's wife, Barbro, who still ran the restaurant.

The wind stung his cheeks as he climbed out of the car and headed for the inn. The door jangled as he stepped in. Two guests were seated at a table, but otherwise he didn't see anyone. He approached the empty bar.

After a while, a large woman came out of the kitchen. Her whole face changed when she saw Martin.

"Why, what on earth... Martin," she said. "It's been ages."

The woman came around the bar, threw her arms around him, and held him tight.

"Martin, Martin," she said again.

"Barbro," said Martin.

Martin was caught unawares by the warm reception and found himself clinging to her, boring his face into her neck. When had he last hugged anyone? He knew the answer: January 11.

Then he began to cry. Barbro did too, and the two of them stood there sobbing together while the guests in the corner sent uncertain glances their way.

"It's so nice to see you here," Barbro said, sniffling. "I've been waiting for you."

They took a moment to collect themselves.

"Have a seat," Barbro said at last. "What do you want to eat?"

"Do you have anything left? It's not too late?"

"No, no, no. Fish stew. Would that be okay?"

"That would be...fantastic."

After a while, the other patrons left. Barbro locked the door and put up a sign, and Martin breathed a sigh of relief. The fewer people he had to deal with, the better.

Soon a dish of fish stew full of cod, mussels, and potatoes stood in front of Martin. Barbro placed a hand on his back and then sat down across from him.

"So what's going on? Sven told me you gave up the farm. Martin, I'm so terribly sorry about what happened to your son. Did you get our condolences?"

"I...don't know," Martin said. "I'm sure I did. It's all one big fog."

"I understand." Barbro bowed her head. "But I'm sure Sven could use the help, if you want to come back. He's said so. That you're welcome back there anytime."

"I don't know," said Martin. "I'm not quite there yet."

Barbro nodded. "Take all the time you need."

Martin's plate was empty within minutes.

"God, that was good," he said, leaning back. "Real, fresh food. Thank you."

He wiped his mouth with a napkin and sat in silence for a moment.

"There was something I wanted to ask you," he said.

"Sure," said Barbro. "Ask away."

"I'm looking for information on something that happened here on Orust in the sixties. There was an ice-skating accident near our house."

He looked down at his clasped hands resting against the tablecloth and went on: "You don't know anything about that, do you?"

Barbro was watching him intently. "No, that was before my time here. But I do know who you should talk to."

Martin nodded. "Elias, right?"

"Exactly."

"He knows everything that went on out here?"

"Yes, the most on the coast anyway," she said with a little laugh. "He also worked for the fire department. I think maybe he's still in charge of their administration somehow, plus it's not out of the question that they were involved. It's a local, volunteer department, you know, folks who respond before the real rescue services can get there."

"Right," said Martin. "Do you have his number? Or address?"

Barbro looked up the information, wrote it down on a napkin, and gave it to him.

The big mussel farm where Martin had worked for years was based not far from the inn. Martin had run into Elias lots of times. He knew he lived in one of the houses that crowded up close to the harbor, and he was often out taking care of his old boat, even if he seldom went fishing these days.

Elias's family had lived on Orust for generations. Martin's had too, of course, on his father's side, but he guessed it would be easier to talk to Elias than to his own father. Besides, Martin's dad hadn't lived on the island year-round since he was young.

Martin lingered with Barbro for a while, having a cup of coffee and accepting dessert before he thanked her and went on his way. He entered the address in his phone and went to search for it among the houses.

He passed several large red storehouses and came to a cobblestoned street. After that, it was too difficult to follow the map. The houses were close together, like puzzle pieces, as if they held each other up against the ravages of the howling wind.

Then he arrived at a white cottage with a red tiled roof.

The sign on the door read HELIN in cursive letters. He knocked.

Martin realized it must have been a long time since he'd seen Elias—he looked much older than Martin remembered.

"Hello, Elias. I hope you recognize me—we've seen each other often enough, but I don't think we've ever met properly. My name is Martin."

He took Martin's outstretched hand. Judging by his face, he was just as surprised at Martin's appearance. His pale blue eyes seemed to need time to adjust to him before he could produce words.

"Yes, sure I recognize you. Christer's boy. You work for Sven—isn't that right?"

"Right. Or, well…I did. I quit."

"And you're the one who…That boy? Who disappeared?"

"Right," Martin said simply.

"Terrible," Elias whispered, looking him right in the eye. "Just terrible."

"That's kind of why I'm here, or, not why, but I…I had a couple questions I was hoping you could answer. About some other people…other people who…"

A shadow passed over Elias's face. He nodded.

"You mean in the same place?" he asked.

Martin nodded.

"Come in." He opened the door and showed him into the hall. "Hang up your things and come on in. Would you like coffee?"

"No thanks, I just had some. I ate lunch with Barbro at the inn."

Inside Elias's cottage, a fire was crackling in the stove. He seemed to have been sitting in one of the easy chairs with a view of the sea, doing a crossword.

"I hope I'm not bothering you," Martin said.

"Not at all. Have a seat." He gestured toward the other easy chair. "I've thought so much about it, you know, about all that."

Martin looked at him gravely.

"So how can I help you?" Elias asked.

Martin told him what he'd found in the attic. About the recurring date. The accidents.

"I guess I just want to know more," he said. "I think I'd like to meet the girl who survived. And I'd like to know what you remember about it. All of it."

Elias turned to the windows and gazed at the sea with a deep sigh before he spoke again.

"I remember it so well," he said. "It was a weekend, not long after my twenty-fifth birthday. My father was on call with the fire department, and he got the alarm around lunchtime, about an accident on the ice. I was there when he came home, and he was absolutely exhausted. Pale. As if he'd just been through a disaster. And you know, I suppose he had."

A family from the outside had just moved into the house where Martin lived now. The ice had frozen, and they were going to visit the islet a way out. It wasn't far at all, a hundred meters or so. On their way back, the ice gave way. The daughter had brought a school friend who managed to avoid falling in.

"I think they were about eight, the children."

"I know the family's name was Svensson. But do you know what her name was? The girl who survived?"

Elias shook his head.

"But I might be able to find out. There's a chance the name would be in the fire department's logbook from back then."

"Do you have it here?" Martin asked.

Elias stood up.

"There have been a number of break-ins at the fire station. It feels safer to keep it here. I've been in charge of documentation for the past thirty years, and I take care of the logbook like it's the child I never had," Elias said with a crooked smile.

He brought over a large, fat book in a worn pigeon-blue fabric binder.

"What did you say was the date?"

"January 11, 1965," Martin replied.

Elias turned the pages gently.

"Oh yes, here it is."

He read aloud:

"*11:27: call received regarding an accident outside Ty- holmen near Ekevik. Group of four people, three of whom fell through the ice. All three perish. An eight-year-old girl survives.*"

"No names, I'm afraid," he said. "But I think I know someone who knew the family. Let me make a call."

Elias took out a cell phone, big and heavy and with no telling how many years were behind it; in the meantime Martin continued to page through the logbook. There weren't many mobilizations a year. One entry was about a grass fire near the diving platform in Kattevik; another was about a fire in a boathouse on Mollön.

He wondered if this volunteer fire department had been involved in the search for his son, and considered checking to see whether there were any notes about the case, but he couldn't bring himself to do it. Right now he needed to hold on to every ounce of the will and strength he had mustered.

"He'll call back soon," Elias said, leaning back in his chair.

They sat there for a while, looking out the windows at the glimpses of the sea visible between the tidy yards and well-maintained facades of the neighboring houses. A cuckoo clock above the sofa ticked the seconds away like a foreboding journey toward an oncoming crescendo.

"They're certainly not the first the sea has swallowed up," Elias said thoughtfully, his eyes still aimed out the window. "The sea has always devoured people. We forget it sometimes, in these modern days when beaches and boat trips are mostly just an innocent pleasure."

His voice lowered.

"In the olden days, it was a real risk every time someone

went out on a fishing boat," he went on. "The boats were often completely open, or half-covered if you were lucky. My own grandfather was one of six Mollösund men who died when the cutter *Andromeda* went down in the North Sea."

Martin let the words fade out before he responded, his voice nothing but a whisper.

"When was that?"

"In 1924. My grandmother never recovered. She ended up going in herself."

"Going in herself?"

"She drowned herself. She heard Grandfather's voice at night, heard him calling for her."

Martin gulped.

"And she wasn't the only one," Elias went on. "I've heard lots of stories like it. It was a curse that came with living out here."

He paused but didn't take his eyes from the sea.

"People just plain went crazy. Lots of things were better before, but not that."

Dad must know about this kind of thing, Martin thought. It must have happened to people in his family too. Why had he never mentioned it?

"But of course, it's not unique to this coast," Elias said, as if he wanted to mitigate what he'd said. "It's true of any community near the water. And even in modern times, the sea still has power—just think of the *Estonia* disaster, or the tsunami in Thailand."

A ringtone cut through the room. Elias answered his phone, posed his question, and listened, uttering a few *hmm*s before he said goodbye and hung up.

"Eva Levin," he said after a moment. "The friend who survived the skating accident is named Eva Levin. She must be around sixty today. And you're in luck—she doesn't live far from here at all. You'll find her out on Käringön."

Two car doors slammed.

She heard voices. The brothers'.

The sound of their steps across the gravel, the jangling of keys, the front door opening and closing.

She could get out through the cellar door now. If they spotted her, she could say she had come by to look for them and had knocked on the door, or that she was looking for a dog that had gotten loose, anything, whatever she could think of. Anything would be preferable to their discovering her inside the house.

She could also try to sneak off. Steal through the hedge and onto the road, down to the car, avoid any questions.

But it was too late. She heard the basement door opening, up in the hall. She heard steps coming down the stairs, the creaking.

Quick as a flash, she slipped into the little room and closed the door behind her.

He's just coming down to grab something, she thought. *And then he'll go right back up again.*

She didn't move a muscle as she heard steps approaching. They stopped by the door. *Hope he doesn't notice the light on in here*, she thought.

She held her breath. He was only a meter away from her now, on the other side.

Go, she thought. *Just go back upstairs.*

He didn't. He turned the key in the lock.

Please, don't turn out the light. Please...

He didn't. He left.

Her first thought: *My phone is still in the car.* She didn't even need to feel for it; she was sure—it was in its holder next to the fan, as it always was when she was driving.

Shit.

She looked around at the foam rectangles, which were everywhere. Above the door, over the keyhole, over the window, on the walls and ceiling.

The mattress on the floor looked brand new. Everything looked brand new, recently bought; it smelled new.

What was this all for?

Her intuition had been a good guide, she thought. The teddy bear—how could it be any clearer?

Had Adam been here? Why wasn't he here now?

What kind of people were they, these brothers?

She sat down on the mattress. Her thoughts wouldn't quite come; she realized it might be trouble if they did. They wouldn't lead anywhere healthy if she followed them.

No one knew she was there.

She searched her memory—who had she spoken with before she came here? Who might miss her eventually? She and Bäcke had made plans to see each other over the weekend, and today was Wednesday. Sure, they usually checked in with a text or phone call when they were apart, but the question was, How would he react if she didn't respond, especially after their discussion in bed that time? He had probably felt the pressure to take a step back, and if she didn't try to contact him, he would likely assume she was doing the same thing.

And he still hadn't met anyone else Maya knew out here, no one he could ask about her in a natural way.

She had spoken to Lia, but they didn't know each other well enough for Maya to report every step she took. If Lia didn't see her for a few days, she and Robert might assume something had come up and she had gone home to Dalsland and would surely check in eventually.

Food, what about food? She had eaten right before she left; that was a good thing. But it wouldn't take long for her belly to be empty again.

She had no coat, just a thin jacket. But there was a blanket. What else did she have?

She had socks, a T-shirt, pants, a plastic bag in one pocket, a photo filter.

She had something soft to lie on if she needed rest. That was good. She had to think positive.

It could be worse.

It could be worse.

It could be worse.

❧

Time in a timeless room, it stops. It makes itself irrelevant. Fades away.

A memory. Hadn't she been locked up like this before? When? Surely her parents had never locked her up anywhere as a child. Then she remembered. She had been a young teenager, and her family had been going to Sunday dinner at her grandmother's house. Her mother had been upset at Maya's choice of clothing when Maya came down from her room. It must have been sometime in the seventies.

"Not on your life, Maya. You are not visiting your grandmother in that short dress. You can see your underpants when you bend over! Hurry and change—we're about to leave."

Her father said nothing, as usual, just winked at her.

But Maya refused. "No, I'm not changing. This is how

clothes look now. You're just too old-fashioned. Grandma doesn't care."

"*I* care. You heard me—go change. Or else you can stay home." Her mom had switched to her police voice.

Maya ran up the stairs, past her room, and up to the attic, where she angrily slammed the door behind her. She had made herself a little cozy corner up under the slanted roof, with an old velour chair and a rickety table. She loved to sit there and page through her mother's old issues of a teen magazine called *Fickjournalen*. "Maya's grouchy corner," her mom liked to call it, since she knew Maya often retreated there after they'd been arguing. However, her mother had no idea that she secretly smoked up there sometimes, because she never came up to the attic. Nor did she know about the hidden cola bottle full of dashes of liquor stolen from her father's bar.

It was cold and dark up there, but Maya was convinced her mother would soon call out for her and give in about the dress. Maya really did want to go to her grandmother's. When she heard the car start outside, she hurried to the window to wave at them, make them come back, but all she saw were the red taillights as they drove out of the gate. She hadn't thought they would actually leave. How had Mom convinced her good-natured father to go along with it?

She fumbled her way over to the door, but it was even more stuck than usual and she couldn't get it open. When she pulled with all her strength, the doorknob fell off in her hand. She sat back down in the chair and turned on the flashlight on the table, but the battery was weak and it wasn't long before it went out completely. She wrapped herself in a blanket that smelled like mold, but it was worn thin and she was still freezing—especially her legs in their thin nylons.

A half-eaten packet of Marie cookies was on the table. She sniffled as she thought about Grandma's delicious desserts and the candy dish that was always full of the fancy chocolates and jelly hearts Maya loved.

She sat there in the darkness for hours, until her parents came home and let her out. She was scared; not even the sips from her cola bottle brought her courage, and here she had never been afraid of the dark. Each sound made her jump—the birds on the roof, the rustling in the walls, the popping of the boiler, the sudden rumble from her own stomach…

She was always the one getting her own self in a pickle, she thought now in the surreal glow of the flickering fluorescent light. Her willful nature and failure to think things through had always spelled trouble, and it was as true when she was young as it was today, when she was sitting here locked in a stranger's basement where she had absolutely no business being.

Hunger, before it has begun to eat at the body. When it still thinks a cheese sandwich or a hamburger might appear at any moment. Before it becomes hunger for real, before it has become wild.

⌒

I will create a day for myself. I am the god of light. I close my eyes and it's night; I open them and it's day. I don't know if it matches what's outside, but in here it is true.

In here is what reality looks like.

I'd like to share a message with the world: there is nothing I hate more than blue polyurethane foam. Surrounded by blue polyurethane foam, no one can hear you scream.

But I can't even say that much.

I realize now that I may never be able to say it, that no one is going to listen to me ever again.

⌒

I remember the apple pies McDonald's had in the nineties. Awesomely crispy, with filling so hot it almost burned you. And the smell...Actually, I think they're back on the menu again. Just one of those. Just one of those apple pies.

Just one single bite.

❧

I've tried to make noise—obviously I've tried. But it's impossible to bang or stomp; nothing happens. My voice, which was so strong at first, it's hardly there anymore. It's been absorbed into nothingness, like everything else is about to be.

I wonder what it sounded like out there last time I screamed, if some of it made it out and was heard.

A goose, maybe, on its way across the sky.

Maybe someone said it: *What was that? A goose, maybe.*

❧

Water

Water

Water

❧

Water

A glass of water

❧

I lie down and close my eyes, turn out the light. Everything is in order. Everything will be fine in the end.

❧

What if there is no outside? What if this inside me is all there is?
All I am

If

All

I am

I am

Is

Is

4

As the ferry departed for Käringön, where Eva lived, Martin leaned against the railing and watched the sun on its path over the bay.

The wind was still strong and wild; it tore mercilessly at his hair and clothing, howled inside his head. Still, there was something freeing about it, being buffeted by the winds at sea—he'd always thought so.

On Käringön he followed the directions Barbro had given him. They took him much of the way across the car-free island, past genuinely old wooden houses with well-kept gardens and to a manor-like building that faced the sea.

Eva Levin had snow-white hair that curled gently around her face. Martin found that he felt immediately and surprisingly at ease in her company, even though he was a bit worried that she might find his visit intrusive.

She put out both cookies and bread with sandwich toppings, saying that it was her lunchtime even though it was past three in the afternoon.

"I've always had sandwiches for lunch since I was a teen-ager," she said. "I've never understood why anyone would eat two hot meals per day. You'd end up doing nothing but cooking and washing dishes."

Martin smiled and gave a curt nod. He was a little anxious that he might have lost the ability to participate in the usual social niceties. That this errand might be beyond him—coming here and talking to a stranger and appearing normal. But up to this point, things had gone well for him today, both with Barbro and with Elias.

In any case, Eva didn't seem to notice his potential social limitations, or at least she didn't show it.

"So…" she began. "You wanted to ask me about the accident."

"That's right."

"May I ask…" she said, with hesitation. "May I ask why?"

"Of course," Martin said. "I understand that you'd be curious."

She gazed at him expectantly.

"I don't know how to…" he began, and he felt his body tense. "Something happened, a while ago…"

"Yes?"

"My son, he…" He squirmed in his seat. "That is, Adam…"

A hum filled the room. Martin wasn't sure if he was the only one who could hear it. He stared at all the blue out there, like blue-and-gray paintings framed by large windows.

How could it be so beautiful? How was it possible?

"He disappeared," Martin said. "In January. They think he drowned."

Eva had just put a sandwich into her mouth to take her first bite. She stopped mid-movement. Then kept chewing. She put down the sandwich, closed her eyes, and opened them again.

"That was you?" she whispered. "That was your son?"

Martin nodded.

She leaned forward and patted his arm.

"So dreadful." She shook her head. "I can't even imagine."

Eva's cat sauntered over and leaped onto the kitchen sofa.

"The thing is," Martin said, "that…" He hesitated again but steeled himself. "I live in the same house as the family you went skating with that time. And from what I understand, the accidents happened not only in the same place but on the same date. January 11."

Eva looked thoughtful.

"That's possible," she said. "I've never actually thought about it. What day it was, I mean. I'd forgotten."

"I found it in an old newspaper clipping."

"Okay then, it must be true. What are you saying—what does that mean?"

"I don't know. Nothing. But it's so strange. And it made

me even more curious. I guess I might be processing, somehow. I want to know more about what happened. How it happened. Who they were, the people who died. What it felt like for you, being there. If that's okay."

He held his breath, afraid he might have gone too far, that he might be taking advantage of her kindness.

She lifted her teacup and took a few big sips, gazing past Martin as she did.

"Well, listen, what can I say? We were schoolmates, Lena and me. We really didn't know each other very well, but there were so few opportunities to go ice skating around here that when they asked if I wanted to come along, I was excited."

Eva told him that Lena's parents had packed a backpack with hot beverages, and they had headed for the islet a few hundred meters out.

"That was as far as we all were planning to go."

It was an unusually lovely day, the sun in a bright blue sky.

After their coffee and hot chocolate, they planned to explore the islet for a bit. But Lena ignored her parents' rule of not going out onto the open ice. She began to show off, saying "Look what I can do," as her parents desperately tried to lure her back.

Suddenly the ice cracked beneath Lena.

"She was pretty far away from me," Eva said, "but

I'll never forget the look in her eyes. How she…was so shocked. As if she couldn't believe there had been any real reason she wasn't allowed to go there. As if she suddenly became horribly aware."

At first Lena's father tried to make his way to her, but the cracks in the ice were spreading rapidly; a hole opened up and he fell in too. Then Lena's mother tried to reach out with a ski pole she'd brought, but when Lena grabbed it, her mother ended up in the icy water as well.

Only Eva was left.

"Lena was calling for me," Eva said. "Or at least I thought she was. In hindsight I can't say for sure if I really heard her calling, but she must have been. I knew I felt the urge to go to her."

At this point, another family showed up. They kept at a safe distance and shouted at Eva. "Get away from there! Head toward land!"

"I looked at the hole. None of them were visible anymore."

Now it seemed like Eva had remembered something for the first time. As if she were looking inside herself as she spoke.

"This sounds so strange now, and maybe it is—maybe I made it up afterward. I don't know. Or maybe I dreamed it—I've dreamed about the accident many times. But the way I remember it, I suddenly thought I could glimpse Lena's face under the ice, her long hair billowing around her pale face. I saw her lips saying the word 'Come' over and over. I felt I wanted to follow her, I wanted to help, and if it hadn't been for the other family coming to my rescue, I probably would have done it."

She paused for a moment, then said, "They made me wake up and get away from the hole. I believe they saved my life."

She took a deep breath.

"I've hardly talked about this in all these years. Like I said, I'm not sure what parts really happened and what I added later."

The cat stood up, stretched, and lay back down on its other side.

"It sounds like a horrible ordeal," Martin said. "Watching your friend die like that."

He immediately regretted his words, imagining that he shouldn't have been so straightforward. But Eva didn't seem to react.

"It definitely should have been. But the fact is, I remember it as...beautiful. That last part. How she was floating around beneath the ice. Luring me down. If that's what she was doing. There are nights when I..." She cut herself off.

"What happened then?" Martin asked.

Eva was still and quiet.

"What?" she said after a moment.

"What happened afterward?"

"I hardly remember. Heavens, there was a lot of fuss for a while. I remember that I didn't have to go to school for a whole week. And that I thought it was kind of exciting somehow, all of it. The attention, the newspaper articles...all the focus on me. But I haven't ice-skated since."

She looked at Martin.

"Then it all kind of came back to me again when that other thing happened. Ten years later, or whenever it was."

"What do you mean? What other thing?"

Silence.

"You don't know?" Eva asked.

"No. What do you mean? I don't think so. When?"

"It must have been...'75. I think I was eighteen."

Martin waited patiently for her to go on.

"It was the new owners, the ones who moved into the house after Lena and her family. It was their son. I think he was four years old."

Silence spread through the room, ice-cold and seeming to hover in the air, waiting for what would come.

"What happened to him?" Martin whispered.

Eva's eyes filled with pain.

"You didn't know?" she asked again, but this time she didn't wait for his answer. "Oh, my dear, he drowned too. Or that's what they think. The boy vanished from sight for just a moment, down by the water, and as far as I know, he was never found."

*   *   *

He hardly remembered the trip back from Käringön, but dusk must have set in, and it was surely almost dark by the time he got back to Mollösund. The humming in his ears got louder, then settled back into his body until he felt like his whole being was vibrating.

Another little boy. Gone.

He reeled down the path between the cottages, looking at their facades, until at last he came to Elias's house. He knocked; he must have looked like a madman.

"My goodness," Elias said when he opened the door in a well-worn robe. "What's the matter? Is something wrong?"

"May I look at the book again?" Martin asked. "The old logbook. It's about another accident. In the mid-seventies."

Elias let him in; the way he watched him suggested he was not surprised.

"Here you go," he said, placing the old book on the table.

Martin sat down and began to browse. At last he found the year he was looking for and the entry:

Call received regarding a four-year-old boy whose mother reports him missing in Ekevik. Rescue efforts are begun but called off two days later when the boy still hasn't been found.

Martin ran his finger along the columns until he came to the date. The year—1975. Ten years after Lena and Eva's skating accident.

And the rest of the date, which seemed to detach itself from the page and hover before him scornfully, playfully.

W hat the hell."
      This was the only thing she knew for certain that
she heard. Several times, at increasing volume, as if the res-
onance were coming from within her.

What the hell!

What the hell, what the hell, what the hell.

Then, after a moment, she could feel people touching
her body, lifting her up and pulling her out. She slipped in
and out of consciousness; she heard questions, maybe she
answered them.

"Are you okay?"

"I'm fine."

Did she say it, or just feel like she said it?

"She's been urinating and defecating in a plastic bag," she
heard someone say.

Then she started to laugh. Or maybe she only felt like
laughing.

Then she remembered nothing until she woke up in

a white room with a uniformed woman sitting by her side.

"I'm alive?" Maya said.

"You're alive," the uniformed woman responded. "We'd really like to talk to you once you think you're up to it."

Slowly she returned to time, once again able to tell that she was sleeping when she was sleeping and was awake when she was awake. Then she remembered her name.

"Maya, what were you doing there, in the room in the basement?"

"Basement? I don't remember."

"Your friends say you were looking for a little boy. Adam."

"Adam. Adam. I don't remember an Adam."

Then she remembered Adam.

"I thought they had Adam. At their house. That they took him. That they made the room for him."

"Why would they have done that?"

Silence.

"I don't remember."

"If I understand correctly, you went into the room on your own? And then the door was locked from the outside?"

"Yes."

"Did someone lock you in on purpose?"

"No, I don't think they knew I was in there."

"So you're saying you broke into the Johansson brothers' house?"

Maya hesitated.

"I don't remember. I don't think so. Maybe it was open. Are you allowed to go into open houses?"

The woman didn't answer.

"What do you think?" Maya went on. "About the room. Why they had a room like that."

"They have a different explanation."

"Oh. What's that?" Maya asked.

"I can't get into that at the present time."

"When will the present time be over?"

Protracted silence.

"How did they find me?" Maya asked.

"It was the people who live in the house. The brothers. They were looking for you after they saw your car still parked there, and they're the ones who called the ambulance."

"How long was I there?"

"Four days, it seems."

"That doesn't seem like so long. It felt longer."

"It's plenty long without water."

Her mother walked through the door. Maya smiled at the sight of her familiar long gray hair, which was in a tight ponytail, and the thick black eyeliner around her eyes.

She tried to interpret her mother's expression. There was not a hint of surprise in it. It said something along the lines of *I've been expecting something like this to happen.*

"You had me worried. What a peculiar story. Why do you always have to ... Well, we'll deal with that later," her mother decided, carefully patting Maya's IV-adorned hand.

Then she added tonelessly, "You're all I have."

The way Maya interpreted that, that wasn't much.

"Thanks, Mom," she said. "I'll explain later. Can you do me a favor? There's someone I'd like you to call for me."

Bäcke came to the hospital that same evening. His face was entirely open, as if all the difficulties and strain were gone, leaving nothing behind but a presence, a love, and she could see it shining from his eyes. It was sadness and gratefulness all at once; she was moved to see it so clearly, moved and a little embarrassed. She had never before been on the receiving end of love like that, much less felt it herself.

Had she?

What had she done?

"I didn't know what to think when you didn't answer," Bäcke said. "I thought maybe you needed to be left alone. I'm sorry."

The next day, when Maya was stronger, Lia and Robert came for a visit with Vilgot, and they got to meet her mother and Bäcke. Her initial uneasiness was replaced with a brightening mood as it became clear that she wasn't expected to suffer lasting effects and that the brothers weren't planning to press charges for her trespassing. But Maya wasn't uncomfortable at the thought of owing the brothers any debt of gratitude.

"So what did the police say about the room?" Lia asked when she and Maya had a moment alone.

They had just enjoyed the meat casserole Lia had brought, since she knew Maya was too picky to entertain the bland hospital food.

"Nothing. I haven't heard anything about their theories. They can't say anything *at the present time*, they claim."

"A rehearsal space," Lia said. "Those guys can always claim they were just putting together a rehearsal space."

"They play music?" Maya said. "Or maybe they're putting on a Shakespeare play?" she added sarcastically.

"What do I know? Maybe they were going to start."

"What about the mattress? And the teddy bear? And the blanket?"

"Just sort of ended up there."

"Ended up there? You don't believe that any more than I do."

"Does it matter? Are you saying you still suspect the brothers took Adam? Why wasn't he in the basement when you got there, then?"

Maya shrugged. "Maybe they moved him when I started poking around there."

"Oh, sure. But they left the kid stuff there, instead of

getting rid of it as fast as they could, before someone happened to see it? Like the police, for example. Or you."

Lia's logic was getting far too complicated for Maya. She
closed her eyes and pretended to fall asleep.

The speculation and discussions continued, conversations
arcing over and under and around Maya; she found that
for once, and to her own relief, she didn't need to be
the driving force or even fully present. No one questioned it when her mind drifted now and then; they
probably just thought she was tired, beyond tired—who
wouldn't be?

In fact, though, it was something else, something unspoken. She still had one foot in the reality she'd left
behind, the one she'd entered toward the end while she
was locked up. Maybe it was death. Or was it paradise?
Or—and this was the question her body kept asking even
though her mind hadn't yet formulated it—was that the
same thing?

At some point, perhaps around the time several of her
organs began to give up, she had passed out. But only once
she was found and had returned to consciousness did she
realize she had experienced a *transformation* rather than
a *loss* of consciousness. She remembered having had the
same feeling once as a child, when she was hospitalized
with a serious case of blood poisoning.

Returning to her body involved the taut sensation of trying to press something infinitely large through a tiny slot.

I could have died, Maya thought. To think that she had been able to let go of her own little self and touch the treasures beyond, even though apparently they weren't entirely hers just yet.

Because now, obviously, she was back.

All she could do was make the best of it. And the words rang through her, words she had read somewhere, although she couldn't remember where.

Death is a stripping away of all that is not you.

Death is a stripping away of all that is not you.

That night, when the visitors had left and the only light in the room came from the constantly humming hospital machines, she woke in the grip of anguish.

What if they moved him when I started poking around there?

She had just been tossing it out there when she was talking to Lia, but what if it was true? That her visits and comments about the police investigation had spooked the brothers? What if they'd had Adam in the basement until her first visit but then panicked and moved him? Or did something worse? Had Maya caused his death?

She realized that she wouldn't be able to get rid of

these guilty feelings until she found out what had really happened to Adam.

Her mother came back the next day and demanded to hear everything, from the state of Maya's health to the basement break-in and how she had been faring on Orust. They hadn't spoken very often since Maya moved there.

Once Maya had updated her, her mother suddenly began talking about Bäcke.

"Finally, you found a good person who truly cares about you."

Maya laughed. "How would you know? You haven't talked to each other that much."

"Oh yes we have."

"When?"

"Well, you asked me to call him, and after we met here the other night, he was kind enough to invite me over for dinner."

"What? Why?"

"We were hungry."

"Seriously, Mom. What did you talk about?"

Maya felt annoyed and betrayed. What had they said behind her back?

"All sorts of things—we sat there for hours. I guess you could say we hit it off. He told me about his life, his childhood, his relationships. You. How happy he is that he's going to be a grandfather soon, and that he had just been going around to look for a decent apartment."

"He's not going to sell the house!"

"No, but apparently his daughter-in-law-to-be let him know they might think about moving to the island once the baby is born. So he's helping them look."

"I see. Well, I suppose they'll need easy access to free babysitting," she muttered.

"Don't be so snide. It must be fantastic, becoming a grandparent."

Maya chose to ignore that barb. She'd heard it before. She swallowed her pride and asked nonchalantly what kind of relationships Bäcke had told her about.

"Oh, he doesn't seem to have had all that many. But it seems a few years ago he met a woman on a dating site and fell for her, but she ended up blowing all his savings, poor thing. It really blindsided him."

"Whoa. Why did he tell you all this? He's never mentioned that to me." It just slipped her lips.

Her mother leveled a serious gaze at her.

"No. But have you been listening, Maya?"

"Don't do that again," her friend Ellen said sternly from a flickering image on the iPad screen.

"I'll try my best not to." Maya smiled. "I just wanted to have a look around."

"You're crazy. What were you doing? How close to dying *were* you?"

"A few hours, maybe."

"What?"

"Or a day. I don't know. I guess no one really knows."

"Oh my god." Her friend rubbed a hand across her face. "Anyway, I don't understand what you were up to in that basement."

"Let's talk about something else. How are things up there in the woods?"

Ellen shrugged.

"Empty, without you. Not enough men, without you. Not enough wine, without you."

"Ouch. I guess I'll have to come for a visit and change all that soon."

"Visit? I hope you're planning to move back to us."

"I probably am. How's my renter?"

"Just wonderful, I think. Our dear Agneta seems to have really settled in. She's got whole rows of seedlings in the gallery windows and bought a bird feeder for the yard. And it looks like she's dug up a potato patch behind the house too. For organic potatoes, one presumes."

Maya made a face. "Ouch. Hope she wasn't expecting much from me here. I haven't even managed to keep her high chaparral alive."

"Her what?"

"The cactus. It died. Dehydration, I think."

"Apparently that green eco-village hasn't changed you all that much. How's the photography going, by the way? Can we expect an exhibit of Bohuslän landscapes soon?"

Maya gave her a secretive smile.

"Not exactly. But there will be something. Things are happening."

"Indeed, so I've noticed. Sounds promising, anyway. But right now, your first priority is to recover. To be honest, you aren't looking super fresh right now."

"Why thank you, dear friend. No one can cheer me up like you do."

Martin walked into the kitchen of his parents' house just as the last drops of the eleven o'clock coffee sputtered through the coffee maker.

Nice for them, he thought, that he was arriving now. They would have their daily pre-lunch coffee to hold on to—something safe and familiar. They weren't made to deal with emotions and mental-health issues; they had none of those tools in their toolboxes.

His parents had hoped that this would be a perfectly normal Saturday morning, he imagined, with a perfectly normal child coming for a visit. Best of all would have been if he had brought their perfectly normal grandchild with him, and they could ask about his car and his work, and the thumbprint cookies would be thawed and everything would be manageable.

They probably wished that they could have a perfectly normal time around the table together, that they could forget what had happened and laugh gently at Nellie as she made her faces and babbled her noises, that they could fill her with sugar and then follow her around as she explored the rest of the house.

But Nellie wasn't there. Because their son wasn't of sound mind, according to the child's mother. She had never actually put it that way, but that was the truth of it. And today he didn't even feel of sound mind to himself. He felt angry, upset, restless—roving from room to room as the table was set and made ready, he let everything come for him, crash into him, as if his entire life came in waves.

There were so many things he had been brooding on when it came to his parents. Things he didn't know. Everything they'd never talked about. How had the two of them met? Had they fallen for each other because they were equally quiet and disdainful of small talk? Or had something happened during their relationship that made them stop talking, and if so, what was it? He couldn't remember ever having heard them argue as a child. And why hadn't his parents ever had more children? The whole neighborhood had been teeming with children, but they had settled for one. Had his presence in their life scared them off it? Or had they simply not wanted more? Why didn't he know any of this?

He walked into the living room, slipping across the newly installed parquet. There was always something to do, a bathroom that needed remodeling or cabinet doors that needed to be replaced after thirty years. It was a never-ending cycle. You didn't have to tackle the hard stuff if you didn't want to; you could always fill the time with something else.

How he had longed for an older brother.

Someone who would be there when he got home from school, who called him into the room and showed him cool stuff or played new music. Someone who told him secrets about girls and sex. Someone who filled the house with noise.

All he'd ever heard was the coffee maker. The vacuum. The radio on Sunday. Beyond that, his whole upbringing had been a study in different kinds of relative silence.

Silence at the breakfast table, where all that could be heard was the sound of his mother's index finger wiping crumbs of bread from the tablecloth. When the toast popped out of the toaster, they all jumped.

Silence at the dinner table, where all that could be heard was the sound of silverware clinking against china, and his father emptying his entire glass of water in one gulp after the last bite. Those gulps.

Silence at supper, when he sat on his own with his tea cakes and milk and all that could be heard was the sound of the news in the special TV room upstairs—with the two easy chairs that were seldom, if not never, in use at the same time.

Silence when he got home and no one else was there yet.

He enjoyed that silence; maybe he loved it. Then he might go into his parents' bedroom to look for something. *Anything!* In his father's nightstand drawer he found a bundle of black-and-white photographs, two men and one woman in different sexual positions.

In one of his mother's hiding spots, on the very top shelf in the wardrobe, he found a box full of old documents. Marriage certificates, birth certificates, expired IDs, a ration card from 1948—a "general dietary fats card." At the bottom were a few diaries.

He never opened them. He held them for a long time, running his hands over their worn covers, before he put them back.

While his mother put the finishing touches on the food, Martin joined his father, who was reading a newspaper in the living room. He sat down on the sofa across from him. Martin swallowed, unsure of how to begin. There was something rankling him, something he needed an answer to right away.

"Dad, why did you call me that day?"

His father didn't even look up.

"What day?"

"The day he...disappeared. Adam."

"I don't remember. I'm sure it was no reason in particular."

"I think it was—it's not like you call very often."

His father put down the paper, a pained look on his face.

"Don't say anything to your mother—she worries so much. I wondered how the mussel farm was doing. Because… because I had gotten a letter. A threatening one. Someone had put it in the mailbox. And the phone rang a few times, but no one was on the other end. It was from a blocked number."

"What did the letter say? Do you still have it?"

"No. I threw it straight in the trash. It said I shouldn't sponsor you, encourage you, that something bad would happen if you didn't give up the farm."

"I got a letter too, and phone calls. I think it was the Johansson brothers trying to scare us. You know I keep some things on their property. Just a warning shot, but I did file a police report."

"Well then, no need to discuss it any further."

Typical, Martin thought. That was it—the conversation was over. But this time he wasn't about to give up; he was out to get more answers.

Just then, his mother called them to the table, and Martin could tell his father was relieved as he stood up and carefully folded the paper.

Martin brought up his question almost as soon as they took their seats. The words were already coming out of him when he realized how unfamiliar it felt to sit there and talk about topics that mattered.

"Did you know about the accidents that happened at the house before you bought it?"

Both of them stiffened, the furrows in their faces seeming to grow deeper as he looked at them.

They weren't so very old yet, his parents, but it wouldn't be long.

"What do you mean?" his father asked. "What are you talking about?"

A car started outside. His father craned his neck, as if he hoped this would provide him an emergency exit, something else to talk about.

"The accidents that happened to the people who owned the house before you bought it," Martin said quickly, forcing his father's attention to return to him.

His father's grim eyes opened wide in a way Martin didn't recognize, and he ran his fingers through his thick graying hair.

"Accidents?" he said. "What are you talking about?"

"You didn't know about the ice-skating accident in the midsixties?" Martin went on. "When the whole family that lived there died? Or that the son in the family that moved in after also disappeared and was presumed drowned? Those were the people you bought it from."

No one said anything. His mother cleared her throat so violently that her pageboy cut bobbed; his father let out an annoyed noise that was akin to a sigh.

"Why would you...Yes, I suppose we heard something about it after the fact," his father said at last. "Once we'd already taken over the cottage. But that was so long ago, you know. The house had been empty for a couple years when we bought it. It wasn't something we really thought about."

Martin hardly dared to move. He didn't want to interrupt the stream of words; seldom did his father say so much all at once. Instead, his mother took up the thread.

"Speak for yourself," she said in a low but sharp tone— Martin guessed the sharpness was unintentional.

She cast a stern glance at her husband before turning back to Martin.

"I didn't take my eyes off you for a second when we spent time out there. Not until you were ten and I was sure you were a strong swimmer. And hardly after that either."

"Why?" Martin asked. "Why did you keep such a close eye on me?"

She hesitated to answer. Angry red blotches spread over her face and neck.

"I suppose it was because of what had happened...It was a reminder of how tragedy can strike. No more than that. I was often told that I was overprotective, but I didn't care." Her tone was defiant.

"Why didn't you ever tell me?" Martin whispered, clenching his teeth as if to keep the pain from becoming visible on his face.

"Tell you what?" his father said.

"About the people who died." He turned to his mother. "I think Alexandra and I could have used a reminder of how tragedy can strike."

"I don't know. I didn't want..." his mother said, tentatively now. "I suppose I didn't want to scare you. Or else I had just forgotten. I had stopped thinking about it. Maybe that was it."

"It was so long ago," his father said harshly. "It was over and done."

A long silence followed.

"Did you know that all the accidents happened on the same date?" Martin said at last. "All three, I mean. Adam too."

They looked at him, perplexed.

"What on earth?" his father said.

"Yeah. It happened on January 11. Every time."

"What on earth?" his mother echoed.

And then only silence.

When he left, his mother thrust a bag into his hands; in it was a little white cardigan she had knitted for Nellie. Martin patted her arm awkwardly in thanks.

Bäcke wanted to pick her up from the hospital, but Maya insisted on taking a taxi so he didn't have to drive. He gave in eventually. On the way home, the taxi passed Martin's house; she had asked the driver to take a little detour. She leaned back against the headrest and stared at the house as it whizzed by, that cute little cottage, the lights glowing inside—you'd never guess what sorrow that house contained.

Wonder how he's doing, she thought. She wondered if he'd heard how her little excursion to the brothers' house had turned out. Although the mussel farm was no longer there, perhaps Martin would be anxious to learn that Maya had annoyed the brothers even more. They knew that Maya was helping Martin out, after all, and maybe they would assume it was Martin who suspected them of having taken his son.

She hoped Robert had spared him all the details of the incident in the basement.

*   *   *

Bäcke was there when she got home, just as they'd planned. He had made a saffron fish soup, and soon after they finished eating, there was a knock on the door.

It was Robert, Lia, and Vilgot. The boy had made a whole stack of crayon drawings for her, and Maya immediately put one on the fridge: a red tadpole person in a bed, hooked to the wall with a bunch of tubes. A shaky YAMA was written above. As the artist went nuts on a box of blocks Maya had out for that very purpose, the adults settled on the sofa, each with a glass of cognac.

"Well, my god," Lia said with a deep sigh. "You're back. Thank goodness."

"Whoa, you all make it sound like I was gone for ages."

Bäcke shot a warm glance at Maya.

Then Robert and Lia told her what they'd been thinking when a few days passed without their seeing her. They knew that she was dating a man on the island, but that was about it. She'd never introduced them to Bäcke or even mentioned his name. They tried to reach her on her phone without success. Still, they had felt silly making too much of it. They knew Maya well enough to be aware that she never felt she had to explain her comings and goings to anyone.

"I still can't stop thinking of that basement room," Bäcke said. "And what they wanted it for."

Robert rubbed the tip of his nose.

"I mean, I don't know if there's anything to it, but we heard something about their sister."

"Oh? I didn't even know there was a sister," Maya said.

"Yeah, she's divorced and lives somewhere else and only visits now and then. But apparently there's been some talk that her children are going to be taken into care."

Silence.

"I don't know much else, what it's all about or anything, but I thought maybe that could explain it."

"Explain what?"

"I was in the same situation once upon a time," Robert said in a heavy, reluctant voice—this must have been a difficult topic. "My sister…She was having a rough time, and social services got pretty close to taking her daughter when she wasn't quite a year old."

A glossy sheen appeared in his eyes, and his face became so serious that Maya feared he was about to have another of his crying jags.

"And you can be damn sure I would have done just about anything to help. I could have hidden her at my house so they could stay together. It was sick, what they tried to do. She was just in a bad place and needed help. Luckily enough, it never happened. Wilma got to stay with her mother, and everything worked itself out in the end."

"So you think the brothers were planning to hide their

sister's kids?" She hoped this would turn out to be the case. Then she wouldn't have to feel so guilty.

"Maybe. It's just a thought. Maybe they were preparing, just in case. A room where the kids could stay in case someone came looking for them."

Maya leaned back in the easy chair and cursed herself inwardly for not finding out the facts before she let her imagination run away with her. With her fingertips she searched the skin on her face, as if looking for something extraneous to pick at or scrape away.

"I've been so dialed in on the idea that the brothers were involved somehow with Adam's disappearance," she said, staring straight ahead. "But this thing about the sister doesn't sound all that improbable. And the fact is, I did see a woman there the first time I was inside the house. I thought maybe she was the girlfriend of one of the brothers. It never occurred to me she could be a relative. I didn't see any children, though."

All four of them were silent for a long moment.

"Maybe he's just gone," Lia whispered at last. "Adam."

Outside, the sky was wide open and streaked, like damaged glass.

"Maybe he's just gone," she said again.

"How can a child just be gone?" Maya replied.

Lia tucked her legs beneath her. "Then again, he has to be somewhere. He's only gone to us. To those left behind."

Martin felt bolstered after his visit to Uddevalla. He'd asked important questions; he'd mustered the courage to challenge his parents' silence. Like an adult. And he wasn't about to stop now. When he got home, he went to the desk in the den and looked for the folder where they'd saved the condolence cards—if you could call them that when there had been no body or funeral. Most of them were the little cards that had accompanied the flowers they'd received after Adam's disappearance. He found what he was looking for right away, a card signed *Uncle Arne*. Martin hadn't been sure this uncle was still alive; he hadn't seen him in years. Apparently something had come between him and Martin's father, for his father never mentioned him.

There was only one person with that name living on Orust, according to the white pages online; Martin took the chance and got lucky. Arne sounded happy to hear from him.

The very next morning, Martin took the car and headed north. It was nice to do something besides sit around moping; he still felt energetic and decisive, almost like the old Martin.

Arne gave him a warm welcome. He was a widower and lived in a cozy little one-bedroom apartment. It was a sunny day, and he set out sandwiches and a beer each on the balcony. Martin tried to avoid looking at the sea and the rocks just below the house. He was surprised to see his uncle looking so old; he was a few years younger than Martin's father. Did Dad look that old too, although Martin couldn't see it?

He didn't waste time bringing up the reason for his visit. Arne was hesitant at first and didn't think it was his place to talk about Martin's parents.

"Why are you asking me? Can't you talk to them, or aren't you in touch anymore?"

"No, we are, but you know what they're like. You have to carve every word out of them with a knife."

Arne laughed.

"Yes, I know—I was the talkative one in the family. Your father didn't say much even as a kid, and it only got worse as the years passed."

"Why, do you know? Did something happen between him and Mom to make them so quiet? And why didn't they have more kids? Didn't they want to?"

Arne hesitated again. "I shouldn't..."

Martin misinterpreted his reluctance.

"Did Dad cheat? Or Mom?"

"No, no, nothing like that. Don't go thinking that. Maybe it's just as well you know. Your mother had a number of miscarriages before they had you. They were both really broken up about it—I remember that. We spent a lot of time together in those days, when they were newlyweds and had bought the summer cottage in Ekevik. They were there every weekend, year-round. I think that's when the problems between them started."

"Did he blame her? Is that what you mean?"

"No, no. She was so confused for so long, out of grief. But she blamed the island. The sea was calling her unborn children to it, she said. The sea was calling. She was on medication for a while, and eventually she got better, but when all was said and done, they hardly spoke to each other. They couldn't reach each other. Your father insisted that they keep the house, as a summer cottage, but he was disappointed. He'd hoped they could move back to the island for good, but your mother wouldn't go along with it. Things got a little better between them after you were born. But your mother was constantly worried that something would happen to you, and she never dared to let you out of her sight when we were near the sea."

After hearing Arne's story, Martin excused himself. He

had to go home, despite his uncle's obvious disappointment. He needed to be by himself, and he'd learned more than he'd bargained for. Now he understood why his parents had been unable to tell him about the children who had drowned. It was too close to their own experiences, the grief they'd lived with so long, the pain that had congealed into silence.

He had to find his mother's diaries again, he thought. Maybe there would be some entries from the years surrounding his birth.

✑

As far back as Martin could remember, his parents had taken the car for a big grocery-shopping trip on Thursdays and enjoyed the traditional pea soup and pancakes at a restaurant in town while they were there. He took advantage of the first opportunity that presented itself. He felt ashamed about going home and rooting through their belongings, but the things his uncle had told him hadn't brought him any peace. He had to know.

His mother's diaries were no longer in the box in the wardrobe where he'd come across them so many years ago. Had she noticed he'd found them, and moved them? Maybe she'd even thrown them away? At the bottom of one of her drawers he found a diary that had once been thick, judging by its cover, but now seemed suspiciously lightweight. When he opened it, he found that most of its pages were ripped out. The few that were left and weren't entirely blank had a pencil sketch on one side—could that be why she'd saved them? Three of them attracted his attention. They depicted a full-length image of a woman, and when he took a closer look, he recognized his mother's features. They must be self-portraits; surely she wouldn't let someone else have access to her diary? Under the first sketch was written:

Aren't I showing a little already?

Martin turned the page and read the diary entry:

Tuesday, November 11, 1980
Yesterday I went to the doctor and they confirmed I'm pregnant. He said everything looks good and that the baby is due June 15. I'm so happy. It's Christer's birthday tomorrow and I'm going to surprise him.

On the back of the next sketch, the tone was different:

Saturday, September 4, 1982
I'm in my second month now. May it go well this time. Am anxious and having trouble sleeping at night. We've had to move bedrooms here in Ekevik because

the waves bother me so much, they almost sound like voices. Christer says I've started sleepwalking again.

The final sketch was from late autumn in 1983, also from a weekend day in Ekevik. Martin could see clearly that his mother was pregnant. It was hard to read the entry; it looked like it had been written in a hurry.

Every night we're here I hear the voice, hear it calling for me and my baby. Why? I have to go down to the sea. The answer is there, maybe deep down. Why does Christer always stop me? Doesn't he get it?

Martin found himself sitting with the book for a long time. Why hadn't she ever told him about this? And why wasn't there any sketch from her pregnancy in 1985 that had ended happily, with Martin's birth? Maybe she was afraid of tempting fate one more time. And had she lost more babies after him?

He realized that he'd probably never know whether any of the miscarriages, or all of them, had happened on January 11. Time-wise, they could have. But the wounds were too real; he would never be able to ask her.

The new, resolute Martin considered the bottles of pills that crowded on his nightstand. A whole pharmacy. It was no wonder he couldn't think clearly. And clarity was what he needed right now. How could he figure all of this out, about his parents and the voices in the sea, if he couldn't get the fog in his head to lift? The doctor had warned him not to stop taking the pills cold turkey, even if he was feeling better, but he decided to do it anyway. He shoved all the bottles into a bag and hid it in his wardrobe.

There was a huge difference after just a few days, he thought; he was full of energy and an intense desire to work.

Early one morning he sat down at the computer and began to google. He'd never given much thought to the fact that there were so many beliefs and tales about the sea, nor had he known that they were especially lively on the Bohuslän coast. Communities there had often been heavily Christian, he read, but folk religion was also strong. Sure, in many of the articles he found, the stories were dismissed as superstition, tall tales, but Martin imagined that they must have come from somewhere. If people believed in something, there must be a reason, a source. He recalled having read, a few years ago, about a recent study that found one in five Swedes believed in ghosts and that the dead could rise again. Folk religion wasn't a phenomenon that had suddenly ceased to exist; it was still around. Like Adam had, and he had, people must have heard calls from the sea, and like Martin, many must be grieving for someone who had been lured into the depths.

There was one piece of information in particular that interested him. Several articles—including one on a website run by the municipality of Lysekil—reported that according to folk religion, there were entire communities in the sea, parallels to human communities. There were even old folk songs that explained how to get there. People lived in houses down there, and there were fields and meadows. Once, a fishing crew had pulled a boy from the sea only to find he had hay in his arms. Locally he was referred to as the sea ghost. And still today, the article pointed out, there were people who claimed to be distantly related to the sea boy.

The story cleared something up for Martin: he wasn't alone; he wasn't crazy. He became more and more eager.

He printed out all the interesting information he found, for his own use and as documentation to convince others who didn't understand. When he ran out of ink and paper, he hopped in the car to get more. He visited the library in Ellös, which specialized in books about the sea and boats. He borrowed the maximum number of books allowed.

And there were also so many other things written about the sea in recent years, Martin discovered as he googled and googled some more. Bold headlines on front pages. Important things, creepy facts. About the climate and glaciers and ice melting a lot faster than anyone had expected. He found an article that proved that climate change had already caused houses to flood in Henån. It had begun.

The sea would rise, drowning shores and entire cities.

It would drown them all.

⌘

These days Martin slept only in brief spurts. He spent most of the night in the office or wandering along the shore and thinking. He often saw the cat sitting perfectly still on a rock in the garden, its eyes fixed on the sea.

One night it came in and lay in Alexandra's spot on the double bed. After that it came in every night. Martin never really liked cats—the way they come and go as they please, and the way you can never really control them. There's no command they'll obey. On the other hand, they don't make much of a fuss—just give them some food and water, and they don't ask for anything else; they don't need love; maybe they don't even want it. Adam was the one who wanted a cat so badly. He got this one when it was only a few weeks old, and he loved it.

Sometimes when Martin woke up at night, he saw the cat sitting on the bed and staring at him. Occasionally she woke him up by placing a paw on his chest or nosing at his face and breathing on him with her fishy breath. He often woke to her abandoned meows. Martin felt like the cat wanted something from him.

"I know," Martin said, petting her. "We both miss him."

One night, he picked the cat up decisively and walked down to the dock. He turned the little dinghy over and shoved it into the water. It was cold, and the wind whipped at his face as he rowed out to sea. The wind was at his back, and soon he was quite far from shore. He dropped the oars, dragged out the cat, who had crept into the shelter of the bow, and threw her into the water. Then he turned the dinghy and rowed ashore. The cat swam, desperately yowling after the boat, but the waves were too high for her and the water too cold, and she soon disappeared under the surface.

It took time, in the stiff headwind, for Martin to reach shore and pull up the boat. He felt satisfied when he crawled into bed again.

Now Adam and his cat were reunited.

The next weekend, Robert and Maya picked up Martin's car to bring his belongings home from the mussel farm.

"You won't step over the fishing equipment while it's on land, will you?" Martin called after them as they were about to get in the car.

Maya stopped short. "What are you talking about?"

"It's bad luck. Be careful. Fishermen used to know that kind of thing."

Maya just gave him a thumbs-up.

"Was he joking?" she asked Robert as they turned out of the gates.

"No, I don't think so—he never jokes these days."

"True, he's very serious. Did he use to be superstitious?"

"No, I would have noticed. But I wonder where he's gotten all this energy from all of a sudden."

"Mmm, it is a little ominous."

*   *   *

It took a lot of trips, but they managed to gather everything without a glimpse of the brothers, for which Maya especially thanked their lucky stars.

"Nice to finally get this over with," Maya said when at last they were finished and unloading the last of the things outside Martin's garden shed. "Thanks for your help."

"No need to thank me," Robert said. "I should have dealt with this a long time ago."

When they were done, they knocked on the door and entered the cottage.

"Hello?" Robert called.

No response, although the door had been open.

"Martin?" Robert said, walking farther in. "It's Robert. And Maya."

Silence.

"I'll go up and check," Robert said.

Maya stood at the sink and gazed out the window, across the yard, and down to the sea as she listened to Robert's steps climbing the stairs and crossing the floor. The sky seemed to contract suddenly, becoming a shade darker. A second later it began to rain, a sudden shower that painted crooked, winding patterns on the windowpane before her.

She focused for a moment on the tiny rivulets, thinking that they looked like long worms blindly searching their way down.

A nearly black cloud slipped into her field of vision. First she saw one bolt of lightning, then another. A few seconds later the thunder rumbled, and soon the rain was pelting down full force.

That was when she spotted someone standing way out there in the storm, and she was almost certain it was him. His long, broken figure, like a cracked and hollow tree stump or like the dark space between two big boulders.

"Martin," she whispered. "Come up. You'll get cold."

"Some weather." Robert had come down and was standing behind her. "He wasn't there."

"I know," she said, nodding toward the sea. "He's down there."

"Where?" Robert asked.

"That's him moving around. See? Down by the rocks."

"No," Robert replied. "Where?"

Now it looked like he was heading into the water.

"There," said Maya. "Did you see?"

"What the hell…" Robert said. He pulled on his shoes and hurried out.

Maya watched as Robert ran down to the water with long, urgent strides; she heard his calls fading into the rain and the distance. When he reached his friend, it looked like there was some commotion, as if they both ended up in the water. Then she saw Robert put his arm around Martin,

218 / SUSANNE JANSSON

who seemed to calm down. After that, it wasn't long before they were on their way back up to the house.

Maya hurried to light the woodstove and put on coffee.

Soon the two soaked men came in.

"Good thinking," Robert whispered to Maya as he pulled off his clothes and watched the flames catch the firewood.

Martin looked like a chastised dog who was still upset he wasn't allowed to do what he'd set out to.

"What happened down there?" Maya asked.

"Nothing," said Martin. "I just...I saw something in the water."

"You saw something in the water?"

"It was probably just an animal. A cat, maybe. I got it in my head to follow it."

"A *cat*?"

"No, no, it must have been a seal."

Maya looked at Robert, who met her gaze and shook his head.

"You shouldn't be out chasing *any* sort of animal in the water during a thunderstorm, Martin. Can we agree on that much?"

"Of course."

They hung their wet clothing on chairs before the woodstove. Robert borrowed a tracksuit, and Martin came down in jeans and a shirt. Then they sat around the kitchen table, drinking coffee, as the warmth of the cottage enveloped all three of them.

"So what's going on?" Robert said, impatiently slapping his palms against the table. "How are you doing, really?"

Martin rubbed his arms to get warm.

"I found some stuff," he said. "Explanations."

Maya saw a flash of skepticism in Robert's eyes as he leaned back and took a deep breath.

"Tell us about it."

The rain and thunder continued to roar as Martin told them about his discoveries. About eight-year-old Lena, who had drowned in the sixties with her parents. About the other boy, who had vanished ten years later. About the strange coincidence of the dates.

He showed them newspaper clippings and photographs; he seemed to be making an effort to be clear and transparent, as if he were duty bound to report to them. But Maya could tell that Martin was consciously being succinct and withholding. That he didn't dare to share everything he believed and thought.

"So you talked to Lena's friend, the one who survived?" Maya said.

"Yes," Martin replied.

"Have you met anyone who knew the little boy?"

"No." This seemed to spark a fervor in Martin. "But I'm

going to try to get hold of the dad. I know his name is Olof Melander, if he's still alive—there are a few of them in Sweden."

"Sure," Robert said. "I agree that this all sounds very strange, but exactly what were you thinking it might *mean*?"

Maya saw Martin closing himself off, withdrawing his entire being, as if he were protecting something valuable. He looked like he didn't trust Robert, like he wasn't sure he could speak freely with him there.

"Adam talked in his sleep the night before he disappeared," Martin said.

"Okay," said Robert.

"He was talking to someone out there. He said, 'I'm coming soon.'"

Silence.

"And who do you think he was talking to?"

Martin sighed, as if he were tired of dealing with people who didn't get it.

"The girl who drowned. Lena. She lures other children to her."

Maya and Robert exchanged glances and let him go on.

"I understand now that she's the one Adam was talking to at night. They lived in the same house, maybe had the same room. They belong together..."

*　　*　　*

After their visit to Martin, Robert called Alexandra. He asked if she was aware how bad the situation was with her husband. He told her he didn't think it was a good idea to leave him alone so often.

Alexandra broke down. Between her tears and sobs, she managed to say that she didn't have the strength to save him, didn't have the resources, that her plate was full just trying to take care of herself and her daughter. And then she hung up.

When Robert told Maya of their conversation, she decided to make an attempt of her own. She guessed that Robert was feeling guilty, that he'd realized he hadn't been there enough for Martin, and he was now doing his best to make up for it. It was certainly thoughtful of him, but at the same time Maya could see that Alexandra had taken Robert's call as criticism; he was her husband's best friend. Alexandra and Maya didn't know each other very well, and perhaps they would find it easier to talk for that very reason. Right now the most important thing was for Alexandra to feel like someone was on her side.

Alexandra was hesitant at first, but eventually she accepted Maya's offer to meet up and have lunch together. Maya suggested a little Italian restaurant in Gothenburg, because she felt a neutral location would be best.

"So he thinks some kind of ghost took our son," Alexandra

said once they'd settled at their table and ordered. She stared ahead at nothing. "How did this happen? How did I end up here? With a husband who believes in ghosts?"

Silence.

"That's a contradiction in terms," Maya said after a moment.

"What?"

"The whole point of ghosts is that they don't exist. That's what makes them ghosts."

Alexandra aimed a skeptical look at Maya. Maya smiled and rolled her eyes.

"A professor of physics told me something along those lines a while ago. He did believe in ghosts. Or, you know, that then they don't exist. If you see what I mean."

Alexandra closed her hand around her messy braid and ran it down to the hair tie clasped around what Maya could tell were freshly trimmed ends.

"Whatever the case, it would make it a lot easier if I didn't have to deal with this right now. It's hard enough as it is."

She told Maya about the help and care she'd received from her parents and sister, and what a comfort that was, especially when it came to Nellie. And she said she'd begun to accept Adam's death, at least, and she believed that she would soon be strong enough to move on in some sense. But she wasn't strong enough to be able to deal with Martin's grief and confusion on top of everything. He would drag her down and she had to consider what was best for her daughter.

"But isn't it strange," she said, "that Martin and I ended up so far from each other in all this? I mean, we both believe Adam is dead, that he drowned. It's just that we don't agree on how and why. Martin believes that the sea lured him in, while I assume it was just a horrible accident, a drowning."

"Maybe you could at least come visit him more often?" Maya suggested. "You don't have to stay over. And I could be there when you come, if you think it's too much to be alone with him. Maybe I can take care of Nellie if you two want to talk in peace and quiet. Though I'll just warn you that I'm not all that used to kids. Sometimes they start screaming the minute they lay eyes on me."

Alexandra chuckled, although she still seemed hesitant.

Maya dropped the subject while they were eating but brought it up again over coffee.

"Ever since I arrived on the island, I've been trying to become a better person," she said. "Physically, I mean, I've started running, but I hear there are good hiking trails too. Couldn't you come over one day and go on a hike with me? We can bring lunch or coffee."

"But Nellie…"

"If you come on a Sunday, Robert can help Martin take care of Nellie while we're gone. I think that would be good for all three of them. And that way you'll have company when you see Martin."

"I guess it might be nice to get some exercise," Alexandra said. "I've hardly been able to work out since I had Nellie, and I know a decently challenging trail we could do in a morning."

"Great. We can also take the opportunity to talk about a project Lia and I need your help with."

"What's that?"

"We'll talk about it later."

"Don't you think Lia would like to come along, by the way? We haven't seen each other for so long."

"Terrific idea. I'll check with her," said Maya.

They made plans to talk again soon and decided to try to meet up that very weekend, since the weather was supposed to be fantastic.

On Sunday, Maya, Alexandra, and Lia met at Martin's house, where they dropped off the children. Robert and Martin took Vilgot for a walk, with Nellie in the stroller so she could sleep.

The weather was perfect, and Alexandra had chosen the Huseby trail, which was certainly steep but was only just over three kilometers long—none of them were in top shape. After a few hours of hiking at a leisurely pace, during which they read every informational placard and enjoyed the view, they took a lunch break in the lovely beech forest. Maya told Alexandra about the book club she and Lia wanted to start. They were hoping she would help them choose suitable books, since she was a librarian, but they also wanted her to join the club. Three women from the eco village had already expressed interest in taking part.

"What were you thinking?" Alexandra asked. "Fiction or nonfiction? Classics or contemporary?"

"Not classics," Maya said. "It would be fun to read some current authors. Novels. The kind you read reviews of or that they talk about on TV."

"And maybe some self-help books," said Lia.

"But none on grief," Alexandra said. "I can't stand all that sugary advice about how to grieve properly."

"And none about needle felting," Maya said, fixing her eyes on Lia.

"Or Miss Marple," Lia joked back.

"Okay," said Alexandra. "I'll make a list of suggestions for our first few meetings, and we'll see how it goes."

Satisfied, but with aching feet, they returned home.

That evening, Robert made dinner with what he had around the house—it ended up being an Asian-inspired stew with frozen vegetables that had expired six months earlier, a package of ready-made meatballs, and some coconut milk.

Cooking wasn't his thing, and he had Lia. But everyone was hungry and ended up sated.

Martin hardly participated in the conversation. He sat with his knees drawn up, almost curled around his plate, the spoon close to his mouth—at times, it looked like he was lapping his food straight from his plate.

During dinner, Alexandra seemed to become increasingly dejected. All it took was a glance at Martin to see that there was just no way that the two of them could sit down and discuss the future right now. Or even exchange a few words. Still, she decided to stay overnight. She was afraid to leave him alone.

Maya's phone rang as they were clearing the table. It was Agneta, her renter in Dalsland, who wanted to give her an update on what was going on in the neighborhood. Maya slipped into the little office next to the kitchen. After she'd hung up, she stared around the room in shock. There were piles of papers and books everywhere. On the desk, on the bookshelves, on the window ledge, stacked on the floor. She riffled through one of the piles, then another. It all seemed to be about the sea: drownings, shipping accidents, tsunamis, legends, floods, images of melting ice in Greenland…It must have taken him days—no, weeks—to find and print all of this.

What appeared to be a brand-new barometer was balanced atop one stack of papers next to the computer.

On the floor next to the desk was a large open backpack. She cautiously dug around inside it but at first couldn't figure out what she was looking at. In the bag were warm clothes, canned goods, a Trangia stove, knives, candles, a flashlight, and batteries. His passport, a wad of cash, and a few documents were in a plastic bag. Survival gear? Once again she realized she hadn't grasped the breadth of Martin's obsession. At times it seemed to be luring him down into the depths; at others it seemed to scare him into fleeing. She left the room and decided to bring this up with the others when he wasn't around.

When she walked into the kitchen, Martin wasn't there.

It was as if they all realized it at the same time—was he in the bathroom? Where had he gone? How long had it been?

Alexandra immediately went to check on the bed where Nellie was sleeping. Robert and Lia dashed into the yard and began calling his name. Maya went upstairs. And there lay Martin, asleep in Adam's bed. With his sharp, naked body in a fetal position, the sheets and blankets twisted into thick parentheses, carefully placed on and around him.

Like a nest.

In his arms he cradled Mulle.

Maya didn't go straight home that evening. She called Bäcke from the car and asked if she could stay at his place. She needed to talk.

He'd made a fire, set out crackers and some fine cheeses, and poured them each a glass of red wine. Maya sat down on a pillow before the fireplace and let out all her worry in one long sigh.

"Did I wake you up when I called?"

"No, not at all, I was watching an old movie."

Maya reached for a DVD case that was on a shelf next to the entertainment system.

"*Notting Hill.* Oh, Bäcke...*again?*"

He blushed. "I love the soundtrack."

"Or else you're the most romantic man I've ever met."

"Sure, maybe, but you go ahead and watch as many serial-killer documentaries as you like, my pearl. Now what was it you wanted to talk about?"

Maya told Bäcke about Martin, how he'd acted during dinner and the piles of papers she'd seen in his office.

"And he seemed to have packed a bug-out bag, like they do in Los Angeles in case of the Big One. What do you think?" she concluded. "You're used to dealing with people that have issues like this."

"Well, I'm no doctor, but perhaps, given what you've described, he could be bipolar—manic-depressive, as they used to call it. With those classic swings between depressive and manic episodes."

"But he's taking some sort of medication—don't you think that would help?"

"It should, of course. It depends on how he's presented himself to his doctor. And by the way, are you sure he hasn't stopped taking it?"

"No, I have no idea. He never talks about that stuff with me."

"Maybe you should call Alexandra if you're worried. She's his closest family."

"Yeah, but it doesn't seem like she can reach him at all right now."

"No, but there's nothing *you* can do about it."

Maya picked up on the unspoken criticism. It *wasn't* her business, but she could at least continue to keep an eye on him.

After their dinner together, he woke to a sound, a call. He realized he was in Adam's bed. The full moon shone through the window.

Aaaadam.

Aaaadam.

Aaaadam.

Maaartin.

Maaartin.

Who was it?

He couldn't be entirely sure this question had truly been asked, either in the moment or later on. He knew only that he had to go there, down to the water again, that there was nothing holding him back.

He walked down the steps into the chilly May night, naked, feeling the rocks against his bare feet, but he kept going, as if something else were guiding him. He suddenly pictured himself as a little boy. This was something that had happened to him, a memory; he had walked like this as a child, alone at night, down to the water. He heard the distant voice calling his name, but he just kept going; he had to—there were calls from both directions: *Maaartin*. He ought to stop and choose a direction, but he just kept going forward, and now he was running because something was chasing him, and something was luring him down; he was there now, at the water, and he waded out, sank into it, and let it envelop him. He suddenly felt very grand, as if he were supporting the sea with his body, filled with the insight that our cells still carry—salt as an indelible memory of our biological origins.

It was so shimmery down here.

He pictured the octopuses with their tentacles and the shrimp with their glowing eyes. He saw a jellyfish come billowing by with its long threads, how it turned around and transformed into the little girl. Now he recognized her, a turned-up nose and a smiling mouth and threads turning to waving hair; she wanted to go deeper, farther out, and he wanted to follow. He knew now where his son was—or was he a son of the water?—and she was the one who could take him where he needed to go.

Come, come, come.

He was farther and farther away. Breaking up, dissolving. At last there was nothing that separated him from the sea, from the only eternal thing he shared with everything else. He did not belong to himself anymore; he had no margins.

He didn't have to listen to the sea or talk to it; he understood everything anyway, with his whole being, how it all fit together. He could feel how the sea was the gateway to purely being, and how its power of attraction was at its strongest when the self was at its weakest, like in a child, the younger the better, or in an aging, deteriorating person, or in a broken, grieving person, one who longs to escape, one who longs to let go and let himself be swept up.

Then, suddenly, everything stopped. He was pushed back into his body, that cramped, limited, ugly thing.

He felt something tugging and pulling at him; he turned around and saw his mother's face, her terrified eyes, and she was so young and she cried, *What are you doing? Where are you going? Are you out of your mind, boy?* Then she vanished, sucked back in time, and instead he heard the roaring in the present, so full of rage that he'd never heard anything like it:

"No fucking way! You bastard! No fucking way are you just going to leave me here on my own!"

Who had such a voice? What world did such a thing come from?

Much later, when the story was told, he would understand the context, what had really happened. He would know that what he'd experienced as an eternity was only a brief moment. That in real life, it was Alexandra who had seen him leave the house, that she had been home that night, that she had woken up and managed to get him back to the house.

Had he even been aware of it? That she was there? Was she there often?

Did he even know who she was at the time?

The words that followed: *delusions, hallucinations, psychosis. Suicidal.*

"I know he's down there," he had whispered to Alexandra in bed afterward. Alexandra, the mother of the child who was gone.

"It was Lena—she lured Adam into the water," he told her. "She lured another boy too. I don't know his name, but there are three of them down there. Three who belong together, from this house. I'm the only one who didn't come—I tried to once, but my mother yanked me back, the way you did just now. You have to believe me, Alexandra—he's there. Adam is down there. Lena never stops calling and luring. She wants other children to play with. And did you know, even my mother…" He stopped.

"What about your mother?"

He didn't respond, would only shake his head.

"Did you see him? Adam? Down there?"

He turned away, angry, feeling peevish because he had to admit that no, he had never seen him. He'd seen other things, other people; he had seen Lena. But not Adam. Not their Adam.

"But I really believe he's down there." And with a child's naïve cheerfulness: "Maybe I can bring him home?"

Yet he knew as he said it that it was a lie. And he knew he didn't want to bring Adam back to this world anymore; rather, he wanted to go to that other world, to Adam.

But there was probably no way she could understand that, the woman who was Adam's mother. The mother who was still a person.

Maya knew that Martin had gone into the water that night. This time he got farther, went under the surface, and it was sheer luck that Alexandra had been there, had woken up and followed him.

The incident had sparked serious efforts to help Martin. He had received medical care and new medication, and he was watched more or less around the clock by either Alexandra or his parents. A few times, he was rushed to the hospital and admitted, but he always came home after a few days.

She had been anxious about what was going on with Martin and what she'd discovered in his office, but she was also fascinated by what she'd learned about those past accidents.

The recurring date, January 11, stayed in her mind like a flickering flame. Surely it couldn't be anything more than a coincidence, but at the same time, being a mere coincidence felt *completely improbable*. Two times, maybe, but not *three*. There had to be an explanation. Maya imagined that someone less grounded than she was might have been tempted to conclude that there was a curse on the house, whose inhabitants had fared so poorly time and again. She was relieved that Martin didn't think this, because it would have been impossible for the family to stay.

She had jotted down the name of the father of the boy who had disappeared a decade after the ice-skating accident: Olof Melander. She'd told Martin that she would take over his inquiries, that he should stop thinking about all that for a little. While Robert and the others thought she was just trying to distract Martin, she really did want to find the father. At the same time, she was convinced that Martin, given the manic state he was so often in these days, would hardly settle for having nothing to do.

Martin and Maya's kitchen-table visits from the winter and spring seemed increasingly distant. Sometimes she still dropped by to say hello; she thought he was looking better. The summer tourists returned to Orust; the rocks grew warm and benevolent again, and the water changed character, becoming friendly and inviting once more.

⁂

Maya woke to a knock at the door. She was tired after having stayed up reading late, and possibly also having had a glass of red wine too many, and she pulled the pillow over her head to go back to sleep. But the knocking continued, and when she finally screeched "Go away!" she heard Bäcke's voice.

"Open up, or I'll set up camp here on your steps."

Maya stiffly came down from the sleeping loft, put on a robe, and opened the door.

"It's Sunday. Is it too much to ask to sleep in once in a while?" she muttered.

Bäcke, true to form, was immune to her whining.

"Good morning, my pearl. Up and at 'em now—I've got a surprise."

"I don't like those," Maya said, "especially on Sunday mornings before I've had my coffee."

He filled the electric kettle and turned it on.

"It's going to be a beautiful day. It's already over twenty degrees. Go put on something that will keep you cool, but pack some warmer clothing too, just in case. We're going out to sea."

"Out to sea? Me? Don't you think I've spent enough time hanging over the water in recent months?"

"That was winter, and it was cold. Unpleasant. It'll be different now. You'll see."

"You forget that I was here last summer. I know exactly how it looks out there, all the people."

"Sure, but you didn't know me back then, my pearl. How many times did you go out last summer? And after all, Orust is the island of boatbuilders."

Maya didn't respond; he was right. She'd never been out on the water during the summer season. Anyway, there was no reason not to try for more photographs for the exhibition; she could bring her camera.

She gulped down the coffee in the mug he handed her, threw on some clothes, and packed a bag.

"You're rowing," she said.

But she soon found out they weren't taking Bäcke's little boat this time.

She was astonished at all the luxury yachts they passed in the Henån marina on their way to his slip. It was news to Maya that he was also part owner of a small sailboat.

"Well, most high-income earners spend their summers on the west coast. But the docks are always chockablock with boats, even during the weekends in high summer. You start to wonder how often they actually pull up the anchor and head out to sea."

"Investments!" Maya said.

"Presumably. There should be a good market for your photography here," said Bäcke, who had launched an anything-but-discreet campaign to get Maya to relocate to Orust permanently.

"I don't sell tourist souvenirs. I'm an artist, just like you," said Maya. "We don't need money. We have a calling."

"Right, thanks, I'd noticed," said Bäcke, who depended on his side job to supplement his meager artist's income.

The sun was blazing as they sailed along the coast with its many picturesque little fishing villages. And lapping waves... It now struck Maya as incredible that she'd so recently considered the sea to be scary and threatening.

Julia was a 1968 Albin Vega just over eight meters long, Bäcke told her. He and a good friend had gone in on it together just a few years ago.

"So who was Julia?" Maya wondered. "One of your old flames, or his?"

"His. Her name was *Anna* when we bought her, and then he renamed her *Lina* and finally *Julia*. After that I put my foot down. I suggested he call her the *Girlfriend*, but he didn't like that idea."

"What a Don Juan... or maybe more of a romantic. You'll have to introduce me."

"No way!" Bäcke said, faking menace.

"Martin once told me he was fascinated by everything about the sea, not just the experience of it but also the biology, the politics, everything. You grew up here on the island, you're an experienced sailor—what are your feelings on it?" Maya asked.

He thought for a moment.

"Respect," he said. "That about sums it up. Respect! My forefathers on both sides were fishermen here. It was a hard life, not just at sea but also in the villages. They were poor. It was a far cry from eco-villages with their built-in heating and automated curtains."

For once he sounded solemn, almost bitter, and it struck Maya how little she knew about him and his background, how seldom they talked about anything but trivialities.

"Speaking of respect, when is Annika supposed to have the baby?" Maya asked.

"In October sometime, I think. You know, she claims she could tell when she got pregnant. Down to the minute. Is that really possible?"

"You're asking me?" Maya said dryly.

After a few moments of silence, she resumed the conversation: "Did she say what day it was? When she got pregnant, I mean."

Her stomach clenched; it felt like a cramp.

Not January 11. Not January 11, she thought. *That would be a bad omen.*

"I don't remember the exact date, but it was in early February sometime," Bäcke said. "Why do you ask?"

Maya exhaled and the cramping in her belly eased. Had she, too, gotten that date stuck in her brain? She was ashamed—since when did she worry about omens?

She patted his cheek. "I'm just trying to show how engaged I am. In your grandfatherhood, I mean."

They dropped anchor just beyond the Henån swimming beach on their way home, and Bäcke set out lunch on deck. From the cooler he took prosciutto, grilled chicken breasts, salad, and some aged cheeses. There was cava to drink, and after the meal coffee and chocolate biscuits that had already melted in the heat. Maya drank most of the wine; Bäcke had his car at the marina.

As they ate, he told her that on Käringön they had more holidays off than elsewhere in the country, or at least they had before. An eccentric pastor named Simson who had lived on the island in the late 1800s had created his own holy days in addition to the Christian ones: his own birthday, the first time he'd preached on the island, and the day he'd recovered from a serious illness.

"Extraordinary idea," Maya said. "I think we should designate this day a holiday from now on."

"Although it's already a day off," Bäcke pointed out.

"We'll call it Grand Bäckemaya Day," said Maya.

They made love in the cabin, which stank of gasoline and winter dampness, then allowed themselves to be rocked to sleep.

It was the best of summer days, like living in a tourism

ad for Orust, Maya thought. Or for love, the love she'd never believed in.

∽

Maya and Bäcke's relationship grew deeper and deeper. She spent more and more time at his place, in the summer cottage he'd personally winterized and expanded in the twenty years since he'd bought it. There was space for them both, and she even had her own workspace there now.

Now they were taking a break in the sunshine alongside the house, with a view of two cow pastures and a cross-roads, enjoying coffee, their eyes closed, letting the chitchat ebb and flow.

"It's so beautiful here," she said. "The Swedish boonies at their best."

They gazed at the land and found that the neighbor's bees were swarming in an oak in a different neighbor's yard; maybe they shouldn't get bees after all—they seemed to come with certain disadvantages.

What about sheep? He'd been thinking of sheep for a long time.

"They also like to escape, I've heard," said Maya. "You need a lot of fencing and such."

"Chickens, maybe," said Bäcke. "I think I'm ready for chickens."

"Oh my god, can anyone ever really be ready for chickens?" Maya wondered.

Fifteen or so minutes later, it was time to get back to work. He went out to his workshop to putter. She went back to writing down thoughts and captions in her work journal—her water project was nearing its end.

When her pen stopped working in the middle of a sentence, she went to the kitchen to see if she could find a similar one, but all she found was ballpoint pens and pencils. So she tried the desk in the living room, where no one ever sat. She found a black felt-tip pen in one of the drawers and went back to her spot.

She'd written only three words when the thought came to her.

It was something about the line the pen made. It was doubled, like a cross-country ski trail.

And time stopped. She didn't understand why the feeling was so strong, but her body reacted before her brain could; a wave of stinging recognition ran through her. She had seen this before, in some crucial context she couldn't quite recall.

She looked at the tip of the pen. It was split. When she returned to writing, she angled the tip so it was pressed together and created a single line.

The feeling of recognition grew even stronger; it roused distaste within her, disgust resounding inside her now. She felt nauseated but couldn't figure out why—she knew only that it was something important.

Then it struck her with such force that it seemed it might cleave her in two.

The letters.

The letter someone had left in Martin's mailbox. *This is your final warning.* She had noticed that the first few letters had been written by a pen with a split tip. The same went for the letter to the Jet Ski club, the one she'd seen on the police computer.

No need for alarm, she thought. It could be a coincidence. Or maybe this always happened to felt-tip pens after they'd been in use for a while?

She went back to the desk and pulled out the drawers again.

In one was a jumble of office supplies: paper clips, staples, pens, sharpeners. In the other were two toner cartridges for a laser printer.

In the third... She could hardly look at it.

In the third drawer was plain old white printer paper—and a lined A5 notebook. As well as a stack of pale blue envelopes.

She reeled, had to grab hold of the desk; it was as if she'd just been socked in the gut. She gasped for breath, for reason, for something to hold on to.

Help me, the words shot through her. *Rescue me. I can't handle this.*

Then Bäcke showed up in the doorway. He took a few steps toward her, until he blocked the whole rectangle of light, approaching as a single gigantic dark mass.

Her head was spinning, her vision was flickering, and she broke out in a cold sweat.

"Are you okay?" she heard him say. And he came toward her, a walking mountain; he was truly a mountain, and she was a lake, a dried-up lake, a speck, almost nothing.

She felt his arms around her. Felt him lift her and place her on the sofa. He disappeared, only to return with something cold and wet, which he draped across her forehead.

"Maya?"

"I'm sorry," she managed to say. "I... fainted. I must have stood up too fast. I have low blood pressure."

He stroked her hair, her arm.

She saw him glance at the floor, at the pen she'd dropped, at the open drawer with the blue envelopes.

"Were you looking for something in the desk?" he asked.

Had his voice changed? Was it missing something, gentleness?

"I..." she said, letting her voice fade, ebb into a whisper. "I don't remember. I just want to rest."

"Are you sure you feel okay?"

"I think so."

"I'll get you some water."

He returned with a glass and set it on the table next

to her. Then he sat down in the easy chair and just looked at her.

"You scared me," he said.

She didn't respond, just sat up halfway and drank a little water.

"I didn't mean to."

He looked at the desk again. He stood, picked up the pen, put it back, closed the drawer, then sat back down.

They sat without speaking for a long time.

"I'll fix some lunch," he said at last, heading for the kitchen.

Maya wondered where her things were, what she needed. She decided there was nothing she couldn't do without— she just wanted to get out, get away from here as fast as she could.

She got up and went to the entryway.

"I'm going home," she said, putting on her shoes.

"Now?"

"Yes. I just feel like I need to go home. I have some medication there I usually take," she lied.

"But...you can't drive. You just passed out."

"I never passed out. Only almost."

He came toward her, put an arm around her, and pulled her close. His warmth was gone; his body was dull.

"Is there something else going on? You seem different."

She quickly shook her head.

"I'm just a little…shaken up. I feel like I want to go home and take it easy."

"Okay."

His voice was dry, hollow.

She left him in a way she'd never left him before, in a way she'd never left anyone before, with an aching love in her chest, mixed with panic, fear about what he'd done, who he was.

When she got home, she went straight to her bed to lie down, exhausted, her thoughts one big chaotic mess in her head.

She was surprised at her own reaction, that she had become so upset. She was neither naïve nor easily frightened. Back when she'd worked with the police, she had met so many people who were cruel, prone to violence, or just plain old liars. She'd learned to see her surroundings from a certain distance, with a healthy dose of skepticism. But she hadn't done so with Bäcke, she realized now. Without putting it into words, she had 100 percent trusted his honesty, his genuine *goodness*.

No, she had to know.

There was no way she could go a single day, even a minute, without knowing; she needed some form of clarity.

So she called him.

She started crying even as she uttered the first words, about the letters she'd seen at Martin's and at the police station, about the pen and papers and envelopes she'd found at Bäcke's house.

"Please, say something," she said when she was done. "Explain to me how all of this is connected. I have to know."

But he was silent on the other end; he didn't say a word.

It would be a long time before Martin realized that Alexandra had truly saved him from drowning. It would be even longer before he could muster genuine gratitude for it. He had no interest whatsoever in his own continued existence and struggled to appreciate what she'd done.

The thing that lured him into the water—whatever it was—had felt like an infinitely more comfortable option.

He hadn't fully explained to Alexandra that his mother, too, had saved him from the water once, when he was little. Had he felt the same way back then? But he hadn't been an unhappy child, had he? Maybe a little lonely, but not unhappy. He remembered nothing about what had preceded the incident.

For a long time he was somewhat unaccommodating with Alexandra, to say the least, as she started spending more time at home after the incident. He was surprised too. He never would have expected that she'd want to have much to do with him, ever again.

But apparently she did. She slowly seemed to move closer to him in the double bed, sometimes running her hand over his arm or chest. Their daughter—Nellie, he remembered nowadays—had started walking. She waddled around the house and the yard, and maybe it was the way she moved, her urging glances at him, and the increasingly word-like sounds that came from her mouth that made him agree to cautiously increase his medication, with his doctor's help, so he could slowly emerge from his bubble and start to relate to people and things outside of it.

One lovely July morning, Martin got up and went down to the kitchen to make breakfast as Alexandra got herself ready and changed Nellie. He took his cup of coffee to the den and was watching the news when Alexandra came in and placed their daughter on the floor in her play corner.

"Keep an eye on her while I take a shower," she said, disappearing again.

Martin stared at his daughter. What was that in her arms?

Then he dashed over and ripped it away from her. Nellie let out a screech that made Alexandra hurry naked from the bathroom.

"What happened? Is she okay?" she cried in terror.

"She had Mulle," Martin whispered, pointing at it. "Adam's Mulle."

"Yeah, I gave it to her. What's the problem?"

"It's Adam's," he said again.

"It *was* Adam's," Alexandra said sharply. "He is *dead. Now* it is Nellie's."

And with that she returned to the bathroom.

He realized the day had come when he could no longer put it off, when he had to submit to the task of entering Adam's room. Had he been inside it even once since Adam disappeared? Maybe, but if so, it hadn't been a conscious decision. But now, one day, he just did it. He resolutely walked in and sat down on the bed. Looked at the pictures on the wall, at the books in the bookcase, at the robe with the dragon head on the hood that hung next to the bed, at the stuffed animals. He could hear Adam's voice, hear him chastising Mulle: *Naughty, bad boy, Mulle, no-no.*

He burst into tears, a deluge with the strength of a spring flood, and sat there for a long time as they streamed down his face. It was as if fresh furrows were violently plowed into him, as if the old ones were regaining their moisture.

Then he smiled at the memory.

He smiled.

And that same night, Nellie got to fall asleep in Adam's bed as Martin read her a story.

He began to recover, bit by bit. In time, he began to cook meals. He did laundry, cleaned, and took care of both Nellie and himself.

Sometimes Alexandra seemed on the verge of crying.

"You came back," she blurted, her face buried in his neck one evening after he'd paced with Nellie for an hour and then put her down. "I don't know if I truly believed it would happen. I hardly dared to hope."

That night they made love for the first time in over six months, since Adam disappeared. It wasn't passionate, but it had a long-forgotten tenderness. Afterward they lay in bed and talked. Martin was cautiously optimistic even as he was afraid that this fragile new trust between them might break if he brought up his Google searches and theories about the children in the sea. Now he had to focus on being *of sound mind*.

Alexandra told him about her visit to the healer and her meeting with the frightened woman at the café.

"The part about the whispering voice seems familiar," Martin said. "It must be the same person who called me and started talking about their awful neighbor. I hung up on her right away. Later I saw she had called several more times."

"I should have brushed her off straightaway too, obviously. A tinfoil hatter, the police said when I called."

"Oh well, I suppose a lot of us are a little tinfoil hatty now and then," said Martin. "Like me, for example, or like Maya, managing to lock herself into a basement for four days."

Alexandra smiled. Martin had come a long way to get to this first stage of self-awareness.

Martin spoke with Sven, his former employer, and said that he'd very much like to start working part-time at the mussel farm again. Sven had long since employed a new boat-man but suggested that Martin could start with something simpler, such as working on the packing line.

They were sure they could come to an agreement that would satisfy them both. Whenever he was ready.

Everything seemed to be working itself out. Nothing would be like it was before, but perhaps they could move on as a family after all. Martin managed to convince Alexandra that it would be best if they moved out of the cottage. That they should try to find something farther from the water. He didn't want to have to worry, he said, or be constantly reminded.

He was afraid he would start to hear calls from the sea again, or that Nellie might, eventually, but he didn't dare to say so to Alexandra.

At some point he had tried to get a sense of what Alexandra thought about the remarkable coincidence of the date; it had to mean *something* even if he hadn't figured out what quite yet. But he could tell she didn't care about what had happened in the past; she was concerned only with making life work here and now, and when he started down those paths, she grew suspicious and nervous.

He could see in her eyes that she believed he was heading in the wrong direction whenever he brought it up. The incident with Nellie and Mulle had shown both of them how fragile his calm mental state still was.

So he stopped talking about it, tried to stop thinking about it.

And it didn't take long for the stories of Lena and the missing boy to seem increasingly distant. The strange circumstances of the date faded into a fog until he could hardly see their outlines anymore.

*

As autumn approached, it would soon be time for Alexandra to gradually start working again and for Nellie to be signed up for day care. They'd chosen the one Vilgot attended, so the families could help each other out with drop-off and pickup sometimes.

It hadn't been easy for Martin to visit his father and explain that he was going to start working for Sven again. Nor to ask for permission to sell the cottage, which was still formally owned by his parents. But without selling it, Martin and Alexandra wouldn't be able to find another place to live; Martin still didn't have a permanent job. His father nodded graciously in response.

Martin devoted most of his time to looking at potential houses and apartments. Martin and Bäcke had become friends after Robert introduced them. Bäcke was searching for an apartment for his son and his family, so they looked together. One day, on Alexandra's suggestion, they went to the big boat show with Robert, and afterward they went out for a beer. Martin felt like his life was slowly getting back on an even keel.

One morning, Alexandra looked at him with that gaze again, the one he hadn't seen for so long, the one that said she trusted him.

"Maybe you can pick Nellie up today?"

A single sentence and he was a father for real again. A dad who drove his pickup to the day care at three o'clock to fetch his daughter. Who received a text with a heart emoji from his partner, asking him to buy something simple for dinner on his way home.

So he stopped at the country store to shop. Nellie was chatting with her baby doll in her car seat. He picked her up and walked inside with his daughter in his arms.

Inside it was like time had stood still. The same cashier at the register, the same fat man in the gambling corner. Martin wouldn't have been surprised if the old lady with the Pekingese had shown up as well, but she didn't. He steeled himself in case any curious shopper were to come up to him, make a show of sympathy, and ask questions, but aside from a few people who gave him quick glances of recognition, no one seemed to care about him. Too much time had passed, other things had come up, or maybe not that many people recognized him with his cap tilted so far down over his forehead. And of course, his dark beard was gone these days.

After he paid and bagged up his items, he stopped at the bulletin board. He was in the market for a new snow shovel for the winter. Maybe someone wanted to sell one.

His eyes passed over ads for a cocker spaniel who needed a new home, equestrian clothing for sale, and a fun night out at the farmstead museum.

And suddenly, at the edge of his vision, there was a notice that made all the air rush out of him in an instant.

It read, *Found: phone.* And there was a picture.

There was no doubt about it.

It was the phone Adam had been playing with when he disappeared.

It was some time before Maya and Bäcke had contact again after she'd demanded to know what was going on. He hadn't denied anything, nor had he confessed anything. He'd just sat there in silence on the other end of the line and at last said something about getting back to her once he'd checked up on a few things.

She had no idea what he meant; she just knew that suspicion was chewing her up inside. Even so, she wanted to give him a chance to explain himself before she took it any further.

But at last, she received a text:

Will you be around tomorrow? I need to talk to you.

They agreed that he would come by in the evening, around seven.

Immediately her body was crawling with restlessness. She tried sitting down with her photographs, adjusting the contrast and brightness; some of them needed cropping. But nothing turned out right. She was out of balance.

Instead she took out the notes she'd made about Martin's investigations.

Olof Melander, it read at the top of one page with a number of underlined parts.

She opened her laptop and started a search. No one by that name lived on the island, but she wrote down the ones who didn't live too far away and who seemed to be around the right age.

Then she started making calls.

"Hi, my name is Maya Linde. I'm calling for a rather…unusual reason. I'm looking for an Olof Melander who lived on Orust in Bohuslän in the seventies. Might that be you?"

"I'm sorry, you've got the wrong number."

The next one: "I've never even been to Bohuslän, believe it or not."

The next one hung up on her.

But on her fourth try, she got a bite.

"Yes, that's me. Who's asking?"

He had a deep and pleasantly rumbling voice, as though it came from deep down in his belly.

"Like I said, my name is Maya Linde. And I hope you'll excuse me, but I'm calling about a tragic disappearance on

Orust in the seventies. Is it true that it was your son who disappeared?"

Complete silence.

"I'm truly sorry if I'm barging in here and opening old wounds."

"No, no," said Olof, "it's okay. I was just so...taken aback. No one has asked me about Johan in years."

"Johan," said Maya. "That was his name?"

"Yes, our Johan is the one who disappeared. I don't suppose...He hasn't been found, has he?"

There could have been a hint of hope in his voice. The hope of burying a body, or the remains of one.

"No, that's not why I'm calling. I'm calling because another boy recently disappeared in the same spot. I'm a friend of the father of that child."

"What on earth?"

"Yes, it's very sad. And...I wonder if you would consider meeting with me? There's something I'd like to discuss with you, and I'd much rather speak face-to-face. If that's okay with you."

Olof didn't respond for a moment.

"Yes, I'm sure that will be fine. When were you thinking of coming?"

She saw Bäcke's car far down in the valley, climbing up the hills. They greeted one another with a tentative hug when he came in; she tried to interpret his body language, the expression on his face, but could not for the life of her guess what he was going to say.

They sat far apart—Bäcke on one of the kitchen chairs and Maya in the easy chair across the room.

"What do you think of me right now?" he asked quietly.

"That I don't know what to think anymore. About who you are."

He nodded, as if confirming a depressing fact.

"I spent a lot of time thinking about what you told me, of course," he said. "Who could have written those letters at my house, if in fact someone did."

He paused for a moment.

"And I didn't need to think for very long."

Silence.

"It couldn't have been anyone but my son, of course," he went on. "Unless someone broke in when I wasn't home, but that didn't seem very likely. So I went to see Jocke. And...well, I was right. It was him."

"Your son? Your son wrote the threatening letters to Martin and Alexandra?"

"Yes."

"Why on earth did he do that?"

Bäcke sighed.

"I mean, I don't know how to explain Jocke to you—you don't know him very well. He's very easygoing about most things—except the mistreatment of animals. He confessed it was him as soon as I asked him about the letters. He said he and those brothers had been having beers together one night—apparently they know each other, I had no idea—and the brothers were talking about how they needed to get some guy to close down his mussel farm. He was trespassing on their land. They told Jocke that they had threatened the guy when they saw him and that they'd called him and his dad at night to scare them, but it didn't help. That was when Jocke got the idea to join forces with them—he would write some threatening notes. For the greater good, as he said."

"The greater good—in what sense?"

"A mussel farm is a big investment. To protect it from ciders, which eat mussels, the farmers often drop nets around them. The birds get caught in the nets and suffer until they drown or starve to death. In fact, a large enterprise here on the island was charged with animal cruelty last year."

Maya stared at Bäcke. "But that's no excuse to send threats. There must be other ways. That's terrorizing people, whole families."

"I know. And apparently he's sent letters to others as well, places he feels have disturbed sea life. Like the Jet Ski club. He's never been all that concerned with how people feel, only animals. I don't know where he gets that from. I've tried to knock some sense into him any number of times, but I let it go when he turned eighteen. I couldn't deal with it anymore. But now, ever since he got together with Annika, he's matured a lot. She's a smart gal, and she's got him by the short hairs. Especially now that he's going to be a dad."

Maya stood up and sat down across from Bäcke at the kitchen table.

"He should be reported to the police," she said, upset. "Plus, he could testify against the brothers."

"I know. They're the ones who started this fight, and they're the ones who sabotaged the farm. Naturally, you're free to report it if you like. But to be honest, I don't think the police would do much about it. Either with Jocke or the Johansson brothers. They might get a fine, at the very most."

He stood up.

"I'm going to go now, if you feel like you've learned enough."

"You're leaving?"

She stood up and went over to him, placing a hand on his shoulder.

"Can't you stay?"

He looked at her with an expression that she couldn't quite interpret, but there was something inside him that had broken. Maybe it wasn't until that moment that she understood what she had done, how careless she had been, how deeply she had mistrusted him before he even had a chance to explain himself.

"I don't feel like I want to do that right now. I'm sorry, Maya."

"*I'm* sorry. I should have…I just reacted. I wasn't thinking."

"I understand. That's the whole problem, I guess. That you just jumped straight to that reaction."

He hugged her hard. She felt him moving away from her, felt that everything was her fault, that she had been far too thoughtless with someone who meant more to her than she'd dared to realize.

She wasn't used to people, to a man, being so important to her.

"Don't go," she begged.

But he turned around and left.

Then she stood at her big cyclops window and watched him drive slowly down the hill and disappear.

He didn't know what to think. The picture of the cell phone turned his whole world upside down. There could be no doubt that it was the same phone he had handed to Adam before Adam disappeared; it had a gray case with rubbery-looking turtle stickers on the front and back.

He and Adam had stuck the stickers on together. Adam had chosen them. Martin and Alexandra hadn't used this phone for a long time, but they'd let him play with it sometimes because he liked to press the buttons.

"Hello?"

"Yes, hello, my name is Martin. I saw your flyer in the store. You found a phone…"

"That's right."

"I think it's mine."

"Okay…let's see. Can you describe some detail from the back of it?"

"It's got the same turtle on the front and back."

"It does! You can come get it. I live at Fyrvägen 12 in Henån. I'll be home for a few more hours."

"I'll come right away. May I ask where you found it?"

"In a ditch along Highway 156. I stopped to take a piss and there it was."

"Well, there you go."

"I don't know if it works, though. It might be totally dead."

Half an hour later, Martin was sitting in the car with the phone in his hand. His hand was trembling; his whole body was shaking.

He could picture it clearly. The landline ringing in the kitchen, his hesitation as he decided whether to answer, how he saw the pay-as-you-go phone on the shelf and reached for it, handed it to Adam.

Wait out here. You play with this, and I'll be right back.

Suddenly it felt like it was all the old phone's fault. If it hadn't been lying there, if he hadn't seen it and figured that Adam could entertain himself for a bit, he never would have answered the landline.

And if his dad hadn't called…

Instead he would have gone down to the water with Adam, and he wouldn't have taken his eyes off him. Would have been a responsible parent, a good dad.

But it didn't matter now. The important part was what it meant that the phone had been found so far from where Adam had gone missing.

If Adam had run down to the water, slipped on a rock, and drowned, the phone should have either come with him into the water or been found on land nearby.

Considering where it had been recovered, it now seemed more likely that someone had purposely tossed it out of a car. Or thrown it in the ditch when they, like the person who found it, stopped to pee.

Which meant someone had taken Adam.

When Alexandra got home that day, Martin was sitting quietly in the half-light of the kitchen. She approached him with worry in her eyes—had something happened? She glanced at Nellie on the floor, as if to make sure she was okay.

Then she saw what was on the table in front of him.

She pointed at the phone with a desperate look on her face, holding out a trembling index finger and recoiling.

"What is that? Isn't that the one that...that Adam..."

Martin nodded. "It is."

"Where did you find it?"

Martin told her about the flyer in the store.

Alexandra sank to the floor, and her wail filled the room.

The next day, Martin turned the phone in to the police, explained how he'd come across it, and gave them the finder's contact info. They told him not to get his hopes up too much, for there was a good chance the discovery wouldn't lead anywhere. The damage to the phone indicated it had been outside for a long time, and it was unlikely that they could recover any fingerprints besides those of the person who had found it. But they couldn't entirely rule out that it might lead to some information about a potential perpetrator's route.

A potential perpetrator.

Martin had never really absorbed this possibility; his thoughts had always revolved around his own guilt about what had happened, his self-hatred. The sea. Nor had Alexandra, until now. Yesterday, she'd spent the whole evening with her head in his lap, whimpering disjointedly about what a hellish abyss would open up if she were to start thinking that someone had kidnapped her son. If she were to seriously imagine everything that might have happened. If she were to seriously start reflecting on all the crazies that were out there.

Because in comparison, maybe drowning in a wintry sea was the better option.

That evening Alexandra developed a fever, or at least she said she had, but when Martin felt her forehead, it didn't seem hot.

The next morning, she didn't get out of bed when the alarm clock went off.

"Can you just take care of it all?" she whispered.

So Martin gave Nellie her breakfast and drove her to day care. When he got home, Alexandra was still in bed, and there she stayed. It was as if all her energy was sapped, as if she had run out of gas. He didn't dare to bring it up with her, didn't dare to ask what she was thinking about. He let her lie there and sat on the edge of the bed, stroking her hair.

At last she said, "I don't feel like existing right now. All I can do is breathe. That's it. Is it okay with you if I just do that for a while?"

The words came in spurts, like she had to stop to catch her breath several times as she produced the sentences.

After Martin assured her that he would take care of everything, it was like she let go of her surroundings completely. Like she had only been waiting for his permission to sink all the way into her anguish.

That was how daily life went for them now, with their roles reversed. Martin took care of Nellie and the household, always making sure that he kept busy so he didn't have time to think. Sometimes the image of the fat man in the country store flashed through his mind. The man with the hoarse voice who had given Adam a box of candy. It made him feel ill.

Alexandra lay in bed with the blinds down around the clock. Soon she began to smell strange, he found, a mixture of sweat and medicine. He didn't know what she was taking or who had given it to her. It must have been in the house, because she hadn't left and no one had visited since she took to her bed.

Martin realized that Alexandra wouldn't have wanted anyone to see her in this condition. He'd called the library to say she had the flu, and her colleagues had sent over some books and wishes for a speedy recovery.

After a week or so he managed to get her into the shower. He soaped her up and shampooed her hair as she sat perfectly still with her arms dangling and her blank gaze firmly on the wall.

Alexandra, you'll come back to me, right?

Then he wrapped her in a big towel and sat her in the wicker chair in front of the TV as he changed the sheets, opened the windows, and cleaned up her nightstand.

When he was finished, he helped her back into bed. He let Nellie sit next to her in the bed for a while; their daughter was the only thing that could bring a hint of life into her eyes.

And then it all started over from the beginning.

Martin was up late tonight. After dinner he decided to wash the dishes, vacuum, and pay some bills. He now understood how Alexandra felt during the long period when he was the one who was out of it. The frustration, the loneliness, the fear of being drawn into the void yourself. The dread that Nellie might be taken away if neither of them could deal with reality.

Even though, like Alexandra, he felt horror at the thought of *a potential perpetrator*, he couldn't help but feel a tiny spark of hope at the chance that Adam was alive....

He got a blanket and pillow and made himself a bed on the sofa in Nellie's room. He and Alexandra were both so restless at night they slept better in separate rooms.

A low humming sound was keeping him awake. He couldn't figure out what it was, but just to be on the safe side he got up to check on Alexandra.

Her bed was empty. The sound seemed to be coming from the bathroom, so he walked that way and cautiously opened the door.

Alexandra was sitting on the little stool next to the bathtub with Adam's blue-and-yellow plastic boat in her lap. She was bent over, and her hair almost covered her face. Martin heard her singing, "Row, row, row your boat..."

Maya couldn't shed the feeling of having lost something whose value she hadn't fully understood. Men had never been all that important to her, she had cockily thought. But it wasn't true. As far back as she could remember, men had found her very attractive, and she had taken them for granted. They were always there when she didn't feel like being alone, when she needed someone temporarily. All she had to do was reach out a hand. And sure, she had felt infatuation a few times, but she had never met someone she'd found irreplaceable.

A friend had once jokingly asked how she managed to attract so many men.

"You know what Henry Parland wrote, right?" Maya replied. "About love missing a cold touch of indifference? It's never been missing in mine."

"Cold?" her friend had snorted. "I'd say it's more like dangerously close to frosty."

And it no longer sounded like she was joking.

Maya suddenly thought of Andrew, the man with whom she'd had her longest monogamous relationship. She'd met him soon after she arrived in New York, while she was living in a dark little fifth-floor studio in Manhattan where the bathtub was in the kitchen. She'd gotten her breakthrough as a photographer at the Venice Biennale, but she hadn't yet established herself in the United States. He was a concert pianist but supplemented his income by playing at a hotel bar near her apartment. She loved his sensitive nature, his long, lovely, pale fingers, and his habit of tilting his head and studying her intensely when she was talking to him. To avoid being at home, Maya often brought a book or magazine and sat in the corner of the bar at night while she waited for him to be done playing. Then they would eat dinner in the staff break room at the hotel, go back to her place, and make such passionate love that the neighbors banged on the floor and the thin walls. Andrew lived far outside the city and often slept over at Maya's.

She had soon met so many new people, both in the art world and at her part-time job as a police photographer, that she had less and less time for Andrew. There were nicer places to spend an evening than the piano bar and many men more exciting than he was; she was just waiting for the time to be right to break up with him. It came one day when Andrew called and proudly informed her that he'd booked a weekend getaway for them. She had other plans that weekend and felt she might as well get it over with. The breakup came as a surprise to Andrew, and he begged and pleaded for her to stay. He'd never loved anyone else, and he'd hoped the two of them would last, he said as he sobbed. Maya didn't know what to say. He wouldn't listen to reason. At last she desperately said "I'll call later" and hung up. It would be better for them to talk once he'd calmed down a little and he wasn't so emotional. But she never ended up calling; she just pushed it to the back of her mind, refused to take his calls, and not long after that she moved to a bigger apartment and got a new phone number.

A few months later, she was contacted by a good friend who told her that Andrew was in the hospital after a suicide attempt. She bought flowers and went to visit him. She had many fond memories of her first days in New York.

When she showed up in his hospital room, she was surprised to find that he pointedly turned his face to the wall the second he saw her. They'd broken up ages ago, she thought—let bygones be bygones.

"What happened?" she asked.

"You just left," he said. "I loved you, and you just left."

"I'm sorry," she said, confused. "I didn't understand."

Only now, after so many years, did she truly get it.

Maya set off just after nine in the morning. She was heading to Lidköping, one and a half hours inland.

Olof Melander lived in a retirement home. He hadn't questioned why she was so eager to meet with him in person instead of talking on the phone, a fact for which she was grateful—she wasn't sure she could have given him a convincing explanation.

Not only did she want answers to her questions, she wanted to experience the meeting, his manner, the surroundings. And it was always easiest to talk face-to-face.

Or maybe she just wanted to get away.

Her memories of Bäcke sat like a big, heavy bolt in her body as she drove. She let it be, let it keep her company through community after community, past city after city, hoping that perhaps it might loosen along the way, be wrenched back out of her, disappear.

Put her back the way she used to be. If she was still capable of being the way she used to be. It had all been so simple. Couldn't she just return, undo? Delete?

When she arrived, the sky was covered in a delicate veil of clouds, and puddles shimmered in the gentle light. The home was surrounded by deciduous trees; in the summertime it must be completely enveloped in greenery, like protection against the outside world.

She introduced herself to the staff and was shown to a section with apartment-like units.

One door read MELANDER, and Maya rang the bell.

The door was opened by a portly old man in brown clothing and a patterned knit vest. Reading glasses hung around his neck. He gave her a welcoming smile.

"Maya, I presume. Welcome."

"Thank you," said Maya. "Thanks for letting me visit."

"Let me take your jacket," Olof said, hanging it in a wardrobe. "Please, come on in."

The entryway opened straight into the kitchen, where coffee cups and a plate of cookies were waiting on the table. Large windows faced a patio and afforded a view of a park.

"What a nice place you have here," said Maya.

"Indeed I do. Actually, it's the two of us. I live here with my wife."

"I see. Is she here as well?"

"Yes, she's in the living room...Elsie?" he called gently, walking into the living room. "There's a woman here to visit. We're just going to chat awhile."

Maya followed him.

In an easy chair by the window sat a woman in a thin, brightly patterned dress, her white hair put up with a clip.

She turned to Maya. Her gaze seemed peering and absent all at once, as if she had a secret.

"Hello. My name is Maya," Maya said, putting out her hand.

Elsie just nodded and kept looking at her.

"She has dementia," Olof said, going back to the kitchen. "She lives in a world of her own, you could say."

Elsie beckoned Maya over with a crooked index finger as if she wanted to tell her something, something only she should hear.

Maya leaned over.

"He's coming soon," Elsie whispered into her ear. "Soon Johan will come back."

Maya looked straight into her speckled, pale gray irises with broken black circles around them. Her pupils expanded and shrank, as if they were pulsating, breathing.

"Is he?" Maya whispered back.

Elsie nodded and turned back to the window.

Was that what she was doing? Maya wondered. Waiting for Johan to come back? There were so many different ways to grieve a child: gradually accepting that they were gone forever, as Alexandra was doing, or hoping to reunite with the child in death, like Martin. Or there was what Elsie did: sitting and waiting until everything went back to normal.

Maya sat down on the chair next to Elsie, and they kept each other company for a while, gazing out the window.

Elsie looked at her every once in a while with that mysterious smile, then nodded again and turned her gaze back to the park outside.

"Soon," she whispered. "Soon he'll come."

After a few moments, Maya went back to the kitchen and sat down at the table.

"It's been this way for a few years now," said Olof.

"I understand."

"It was difficult at first, but eventually you get used to it. We'll see how long it works. I don't think she's unhappy, anyway. Please, help yourself." He gestured at the table.

"Thank you," Maya said.

"So," said Olof. "What's on your mind?"

Maya lowered her voice a notch to spare Elsie from being forced to listen to their conversation if she didn't want to.

"Like I said on the phone, I have this friend, Martin, who lives in the house on Orust you owned in the seventies. His parents bought it from you, according to the documents we found."

Olof just looked at her, apparently waiting for her to continue.

"And earlier this year, his three-year-old son, Adam, disappeared down by the sea. The body was never found, but his bucket and one shoe were recovered from the water. Unfortunately, all signs seem to indicate that he drowned."

Olof's gaze was deep and serious, but there was a gentleness in his face that Maya guessed was an active choice, a gentleness that had to be tended and defended by anyone who had faced real challenges in life. She found herself hoping she would someday see it in Alexandra's and Martin's faces.

"Yes, I heard about that on the radio, I realized after we spoke. Obviously I'd hoped he'd been found."

"I'm sorry if I'm reopening old wounds…"

Olof shook his head. "It's okay."

He stood up and went over to a tall bureau with several framed photographs on top.

"This is what Johan looked like," he said. "This picture was taken right before Christmas, just a few weeks before he disappeared. He had just turned four."

The boy in the black-and-white photograph was looking at the camera. It could have been Olof himself as a child— the same deep, serious gaze.

"You look alike," Maya said softly.

"So they say," said Olof.

"Adam's father has come across some pretty strange details surrounding Adam's disappearance. That's really why I'm here, to help him figure them out so he can find some peace of mind."

"What kind of strange details?" Olof asked.

"It's about the date," Maya said. "I don't know if you

knew that a whole family had died on an ice-skating trip a decade earlier?"

"Yes, I'm aware of that."

"Well, all three accidents happened on the same date. January 11. It's really baffling. I just wanted to find out if you…I don't know. If you had any thoughts about that."

Olof put down his coffee cup and sat, leaning back in his chair as if he were letting the question sink in.

"Well, you know, I can explain why our son disappeared on that particular date. My wife always went down to honor that family of ice-skaters on January 11, because that was when they died. We would place flowers in the water and so on."

He paused.

"And then… well. She was alone with Johan that time—I was working—and she took her eyes off him for a moment. When she looked up again, he was gone. It only took a second."

Maya wasn't sure she understood what Olof was saying. *Is it that simple?*

"We could hardly stand to be in the house after that," Olof said. "And a few years later, we sold it. But Lilly kept visiting the spot on the anniversary, every year."

"Lilly?"

"Yes—my wife at the time. We got divorced a few years later."

"So Elsie…" Maya said, pointing toward the living room in confusion. "Elsie isn't Johan's mother?"

Olof gave a dry little laugh.

"Oh yes, she is, but not the same Johan."

He didn't say anything for a moment, and then: "We had a son together and named him Johan too. He's married and lives in London, but he comes for a visit sometimes. She's always sitting at the window and waiting for him."

Maya's head was spinning. So Elsie wasn't the grieving one here—that was Olof. And he hadn't just sat passively, waiting for everything to be okay. Far from it— he had gotten himself not only a new wife but also a new Johan.

Maya found herself at a loss. She no longer knew what she wanted to ask or why.

They chatted about other things for a while. Then she picked up a thread that felt urgent, but she hadn't prepared him for it and wasn't sure of the kindest way to ask.

"Do you remember if Johan acted strangely at all before he disappeared?"

Olof's back was perfectly straight already, but he seemed to sit up even taller at her question, as if he were using his body as a shield, as defense against something unwelcome.

"Before he disappeared? I don't quite understand. What do you mean?"

A slight shift flickered over his face, a shift that

encompassed long-restrained wonder, and perhaps fear or doubt.

"Did he sleepwalk or seem to be talking to someone, anything like that?"

At first Olof didn't move at all, but then he shook his head almost imperceptibly even as his thoughts seemed to be somewhere else entirely.

"I…" he began, looking up. "I can't—I'm afraid I need to go lie down and rest for a while, if you'll excuse me. It's my heart, I…"

"Of course. I was just about to leave."

Maya stood up and put on her jacket. A hasty idea finally settled into place among her chaotic thoughts and made her stop short.

"Just one thing."

"Sure."

"You said Lilly kept coming to the place where Johan disappeared, on the anniversary?"

He looked relieved and seemed to perk up now that he realized she wasn't going to stay or insist that he respond to her earlier question.

"Yes, as long as we were married, anyway. After that, I don't know. After Johan drowned, it was like I no longer existed in her world—we had nothing to say to each other. She had God and the dog; I had nothing. At last we got a divorce. We haven't been in touch for many, many years."

"You have no idea what she's doing these days?"

"I heard she had moved back to the area. So it's not out of the question that she still goes there each year on the day. That would be like her. She had a hard time letting go and moving on."

Maya stared at Olof.

"She moved back to Orust? And she was in the habit of visiting the place of his disappearance on January 11?"

Olof Melander nodded, looking gray and confused, as if he were too old and tired to understand where her thoughts were leading her.

As soon as she was outside of the retirement home, she took out her phone for a new search of the white pages. Apparently Lilly had never changed her last name—there was an L. Melander listed on Orust. The age was about right. That had to be her, Maya thought.

She wondered how best to proceed.

Should she just drive out there, make up some reason for her visit, and hope to be able to chat with Lilly? Should she contact Martin and Alexandra? Or was it a better idea to call Robert and Lia? She didn't want to reopen any more wounds; she didn't want to get Martin's and Alexandra's hopes up if she turned out to be wrong.

Wrong about what?

What did she think she would find?

She pictured a woman sitting down by the beach on the anniversary of her son's disappearance.

A little boy suddenly wanders down alone; he looks to be about the same age as her own Johan when he vanished all those years ago, so long ago and yet so close, so close to her heart.

Maybe it was almost like this was meant to be. As if some higher power wanted to set things right.

A child who would soon forget—it happens so fast at that age. Maybe she just wanted to borrow him for a while.

Maya stopped outside Vänersborg and ate a hamburger. Then she got back on the road and was in Orust by four. She had planned to go straight home. But she couldn't let it go.

She entered Lily's address into her phone and began thinking up excuses for a visit, ones that wouldn't seem too odd. Maybe she should just tell the truth, that she was looking into the circumstances surrounding Adam's disappearance and was hoping to speak to others who had experienced incidents at the same place. She could even mention that she had spoken to Lilly's ex-husband.

According to the map, Lilly's house was in a secluded spot in the woods. It wasn't far now, just three minutes away.

She turned onto a smaller road with a PRIVATE sign and after a hundred meters or so arrived at a well-kept little cottage with hollyhocks blooming at one corner. One window was illuminated.

Can this be where she lives? Maya thought, getting out of the car. It certainly seemed like a house that would suit an older woman. Or a young, cocky guy, for that matter, she admonished herself; she was always struggling to rid herself of preconceived notions about other people.

She looked around. No car was in sight, but behind the house she could glimpse a building that might serve as a garage.

There was no nameplate on the door; no one opened it when she rang the bell, and she couldn't hear any movement inside. She would have to try again another time.

She told herself that this was just her imagination working overtime again; this Lilly was probably just a solitary, God-fearing old woman.

Disappointed, she got back in the car and turned homeward. At least she had a pleasant evening to look forward to. The book circle was going to meet at Lia's house. Unfortunately Alexandra probably wouldn't be there, because according to Robert, she had completely fallen apart after the phone was recovered. She hadn't heard from Martin for a long time; after all, he was no longer on his own.

Martin was on his way to pick up Nellie at day care when Alexandra's mother called to say that she and Alexandra's dad were in the neighborhood and would be happy to pick up Nellie for him, if he didn't mind. Afterward they could make dinner together. And by the way, how was Alexandra doing? she wondered. Alexandra hadn't been answering her phone recently and only sent the occasional brief text.

Martin was just passing the country store when he got the call, so he stopped in the parking lot to speak undisturbed.

He decided to tell Alexandra's mother what was going on. Perhaps it was a hasty decision—he wasn't sure; it felt like she had caught him off guard. He said there probably wasn't any reason to worry yet, that Alexandra's behavior must just be a delayed reaction to everything she'd been through, all the responsibility she'd had to take on for so long.

It was silent on the other end. Alexandra's mother couldn't have been expecting this. Surely she had been under the impression that Alexandra, the stable and industrious partner in their marriage, was still the one coping best. Last time they'd seen each other, it must have seemed like Alexandra had come through the worst of this crisis.

"We'll pick up Nellie and come over to make dinner," she said firmly, sounding almost stern. "See you later."

He texted Alexandra so she could prepare herself for the surprise visit, or just so at least she couldn't get after him about it. She didn't respond.

Then he sat in the car for a long time, until at last he decided to go in and do some shopping while he was there.

The door dinged as he walked in, and the warm air enveloped him. He made his usual route: dairy, diapers, bread, canned goods, vegetables. Then he headed for the candy section and wondered if there was anything else he needed.

As he approached the register, he heard the voice of the employee there, words that stopped him in his tracks for a moment before he figured out why.

"Well, what have we here?" she said brightly. "Pancakes and chocolate pudding again. I'll have to try that combo myself sometime."

Slowly he looked up. There were several people ahead of

him in line. He couldn't get a clear view of the person who was currently paying and bagging their purchases.

Pancakes and chocolate pudding. That had been Adam's favorite.

At first he was merely filled with a great angst, but then something else crept over him—an icy feeling followed by an incredible thought.

Once the customer had paid, she went to the gambling corner to get her dog. And then Martin realized who she was.

The old lady with the Pekingese.

For a moment, he was paralyzed. Then he acted without thinking. As the woman left the store, he got out of line and discreetly set his basket in a corner. One of the customers, an older man, saw what he was doing and was about to speak up, but Martin couldn't explain himself, couldn't worry about anyone else right now.

He hurried to his car, keeping out of sight of the woman with the dog.

When she drove off, he followed.

Unnoticeably, as if he didn't exist.

He was afraid she would discover him, so he trailed her car at such a distance that he was afraid he had lost her at several points. All along, thoughts were darting through his mind like fugitives: What was he doing? What was he

288 / SUSANNE JANSSON

thinking? She had bought pancakes and chocolate pudding, a treat Adam had liked; why should that mean anything?

Why not?

What if. *What if it did?*

His good sense was trying to talk him out of it, but these days his good sense was a flabby muscle. So instead of aborting the mission, he pressed on, his hands squeezing the wheel harder and harder. What did he have to lose?

When the woman suddenly stopped outside a cobbler's shop and left the car, taking the dog with her, Martin had a chance to gather his thoughts and reconsider. What would he do when she got where she was going? She was an old lady, probably single; surely she wouldn't open the door to a strange man. Not even if she recognized him from the store—but he wasn't sure if she had ever seen him there, or if she had seen only Adam. She would probably ignore him. He thought of Maya, who was good with people when she wanted to be, and decided it would look much better if he were in the company of a middle-aged woman. If he was lucky, she would agree to come with him right away, but otherwise he could follow this woman now and write down her address so he and Maya could drive over together at a later date.

Maya didn't answer when he called, but he left a message on her voicemail. He gave a brief explanation of where he was, saying that he was following a car driven by a suspicious older woman and needed Maya's help right away. He would call again as soon as he knew the woman's address. It wasn't long before Maya texted back: OK.

The woman came out of the cobbler's, and Martin resumed following her, down roads that grew narrower and emptier. He fixed his eyes on the taillights; they danced in his vision like tiny red dots far ahead. His heart was pounding. Soon he would no longer be able to follow her undetected.

At last she turned onto a road with a PRIVATE sign, and he kept going straight. Then he drove into the woods and parked, doubling back on foot and hoping that it wouldn't be far.

He wasn't dressed for a walk in the forest on such a chilly evening; he was wearing a light fall jacket and sneakers. Soon he could feel the moisture seeping up between his toes from the soggy ground.

He got lucky, and after only a few minutes he could see a building through the trees: a little one-and-a-half-story cottage with horizontal brown siding and a black roof.

The woman opened the door and walked into the house.

A memory flickered to life in Martin's brain when he saw the Pekingese. Something he'd repressed. *The cat!* Fillyjonk. If Adam came home again, how could he tell him the truth? No, it was unimaginable; he would lose his son again. Not even Alexandra knew; she thought the cat had run away or that a fox had gotten her. They would have to make it up to Adam somehow. A puppy, maybe—hadn't he always dreamed of having one? And if it was real, the idea that Martin had gotten into his head, that Adam had been living in this house since he disappeared, wouldn't he probably miss the dog when he came home?

Martin forced the terrible memory from his mind. He'd been sick back then, confused, he assured himself, and he had meant well.

After sending Maya a text with his location, he turned off the sound on his phone so it wouldn't give him away.

Now he was thankful for the darkness settling around him; there was no chance that the woman inside would be able to spot him among the trees on the other side of the road. Yet he had a clear view of her and could see her moving from room to room. He reminded himself that she must not spot him before Maya arrived, but by now he was so agitated he couldn't just stand around doing nothing. He decided to just take a quick peek inside and then go back to the car to wait.

He sneaked up to the house and leaned against it, closing his eyes and taking a few deep breaths, praying to a god he didn't believe in. Then he opened his eyes, turned toward the window, and found himself staring right into what appeared to be the woman's living room. There was a TV in it. The woman walked over and turned it on.

She channel surfed until she found a kids' show. Then she left the room.

What happened next was so extraordinary that Martin's legs simply gave way; he couldn't absorb the sight that met his eyes.

A boy walked into the room. A boy who looked just like Adam.

That was his first thought: a boy who looked just like Adam.

The boy sat down on the floor in front of the TV, just a few meters from Martin; he was looking at the boy in profile. The dog came over and lay down beside the boy, who ran his hand over her fur.

The boy who looked like Adam.

The boy who was Adam.

That was Adam.

That was his son.

Of course it was his son.

Not quite aware of what he was doing, he approached the window until he was right up next to the pane. Perhaps he was so close that he rested his forehead against it. Perhaps he made some sound, because Adam turned his head and looked right at him.

For a long time he stood there, just like that, staring into his son's eyes. He couldn't bring himself to move; he couldn't think; he couldn't do a thing.

Time dissolved; everything around him dissolved. Then he heard sounds behind him, maybe steps, maybe a stick cracking. But time was moving so slowly, and his body was paralyzed. He couldn't even manage to turn around before something hard struck him in the head and everything went black.

M aya had hopped in the car the moment she heard Martin's voicemail. She had immediately concluded that the older woman he had mentioned was Lilly Melander. Had Martin talked to Olof too? How else would this have happened?

The roads leading to the house were deserted, but now, as she turned onto a narrower one, she met a car coming the other way. She stopped at the side of the road to give it room to pass, and despite the darkness, she could tell that the driver was an older woman.

She made a note of the license-plate number in her phone. Maya's vision was swimming, her skin crawling.

She longed to call Bäcke, hear his voice, be embraced by the warmth and security he radiated, but she quashed the impulse and drove on. When she came to the private drive, she turned off the road and approached the cottage. Like the last time she was here, one window was aglow, but the house was otherwise dark.

A flock of crows took off from a tree, the sound of their wingbeats filling the air.

Then she heard another sound, a whimper.

Maya looked around and discovered a man lying on the ground beneath a window. As she approached, he struggled to sit up, using the cottage as a support, and gazed her way with vacant eyes.

"Martin?" she said. "Is that you, Martin? What happened?"

Waking up on January 11 was always special. In the early years, the date had cut through her chest like knives, but recently she had found some peace in its recurrence, as if it were the only constant left in her life now. More than forty years had passed since it happened; he would have been a middle-aged man now, her Johan. She might have been a grandmother.

She had developed a routine for this day, something to hold on to that would call forth the memory of Johan and help her believe that he truly had existed.

First she placed his portrait on the kitchen table. Then she set out the same breakfast they had eaten the day he disappeared: cornflakes with filmjölk and toast with soft cheese from a tube. Then she imagined that he was sitting there, that she was talking to him the way you talk to a four-year-old.

Shall I cut your crusts off?

Do you want more milk?

She made a pot of coffee, transferred it to a Thermos, and tucked it into the picnic basket along with a packet of vanilla cookies. A blanket, too, to sit on, maybe wrap around herself, in case it was chilly.

Her heart was light as she drove to *the spot*, as she called it—short and sweet. That was what had happened over the years: sometimes she was able to experience the day as a solemn occasion but without feeling any grief. As if it brought more of an airy feeling of something grand, something meaningful that lifted her spirits once a year and buoyed her through what was otherwise a largely meaningless existence.

She had Lisa, of course. She'd always had a Lisa, all these years, and each time she died, she got a new Pekingese, which she also named Lisa.

Ever since she was a child, she'd imagined she would one day have a daughter named Lisa.

Johan and Lisa.

That was how she'd pictured her future family when she was younger: Lilly and Olof, Johan and Lisa. But then she had turned thirty and they'd been trying for a decade and she still wasn't pregnant, so she had tried to make peace with the idea that she might never have children.

It didn't work. Perhaps she could live without two of them, a Johan and a Lisa, but was she going to be robbed of them both? While her friends' families continued to grow?

And the more they grew, the more they seemed to close off, until they disappeared into an unfamiliar and unreachable sphere of their own. Olof couldn't understand; he took life as it came, thought they were doing fine together, just the two of them. Quiet and pleasant. She had begun to feel increasingly lonely and increasingly bitter. That was when she bought her first Pekingese and named her Lisa. To comfort herself? Or to wave a white flag at God: *I have accepted that I will never have a child?* She wasn't sure.

And then, at last, the miracle happened.

She woke one morning and felt nauseated, had to run to the bathroom to throw up. Still, it didn't hit her until Olof suggested that evening that she might be pregnant. She had hoped so many times that her period wouldn't come that she had used up all her reserves. And now... yes, it must be at least a week late, she realized, just like that.

They had bought the house on Orust much earlier, as a vacation home, when they still took it for granted that they would have a family, as a matter of course. But without children, everything about the place felt incomplete.

And suddenly it all felt so *for real*, their life.

The fluttering she could soon feel in her belly turned into a little boy, and now Lilly could kneel, weeding, with the stroller beside her, could listen to Johan waking up, grab the handle, and jostle it a little until he fell back to sleep.

Now she could plant strawberries in the ground and

know that she wouldn't be the only one to taste them at Midsummer; there would be her child too.

Now she could get in touch with old friends again; she was *Mama*, a full-fledged woman. She was one of them.

And now she could calmly await her daughter, Lisa.

She would have to pick a different name for the next dog, she cheerfully thought. It wouldn't do for a daughter to share a name with the Pekingese. She was sure it would be a funny story to tell her friends later.

But Johan turned four, and she still hadn't gotten pregnant again.

Sometimes, afterward, she thought she had allowed him to mean too much and that was why he had disappeared. That God made sure he went back to whatever place of origin he'd come from in the first place. That Johan might have longed to go back, that he hadn't wanted to be with her and Olof.

All sorts of thoughts came to her.

She'd heard about the skating accident before, but only once Johan was born and they decided to move to Orust permanently did she begin to feel that they should honor the family who had previously lived in their house, who had lost their lives. It was probably something about life and death, how it might eventually become a lovely opportunity to reflect over those kinds of questions with Johan, a tradition.

So each year on January 11, they went down to the sea and had a picnic and placed flowers in the water; most years they lucked out on the weather. Sometimes Olof joined them; sometimes he didn't.

The year when Johan was four, it was just the two of them. Olof was off working at the job he'd gotten at a shipyard on the island of Tjörn. She had bought three gerbera daisies: one for the ill-fated mother, one for the father, and one for little Lena. They were lying loose in the basket, gently tucked inside the blanket so they wouldn't freeze, as Johan had said.

Then they went down to the water.

She hadn't even been doing anything in particular. She was just sitting on the big stump and gazing at the sea as Johan walked around throwing rocks in the water. She had let her mind drift for a moment, thinking of the little girl and her parents and how quickly it could happen, how fragile life was.

Then she heard a distant splash, louder than those from the rocks Johan had been throwing.

She wasn't able to determine where the sound had come from, and at the same time, she realized that she could no longer see her son.

No more than a few seconds had passed, or maybe it had been half a minute, because he'd been right next to her.

A minute, max.

But now she couldn't see him.

It was strange; she had a view of the entire rocky beach and the narrow wooden jetty that ran along the rocks and all the way to the big, smooth boulder with its ladder into the water.

Was he on the other side?

She rounded the tall rocks, but there was no Johan there either.

She called out.

No response.

Eventually tons of people showed up to search for him, but she never saw her son again, not even his body. He was just gone, leaving behind an eternal void that never left her side from that day forward.

How can you survive with a void at your side?

It was over between her and Olof after that; they lived separate lives even though they resided in the same house. Even back when Johan was born, it was as if all her love transferred to the baby while Olof faded into the background. In moments of self-awareness she was able to admit to herself that her main reason for getting married was to have children. Without Johan she could no longer fool herself or Olof. They moved back to Lidköping, and soon he was completely out of her life. They had sold the cottage on Orust by then, and one day he remarked that they should probably live separately since he had met another woman and intended to be with her now. It was all the same to Lilly; in fact, if anything, she could better live her grief, find more healing, when he wasn't around.

Lilly rented a one-bedroom apartment and got a job at a gas station on the outskirts of Lidköping. But each year, on January 11, she went to the spot on Orust and drank coffee and placed flowers in the water, four of them now. Typically she stayed for a few days, taking a room at a guesthouse, and in time she came to form a new connection to the island that had taken her only child.

The void at her side somehow seemed more intimate here, less frightening, as if it were filled in somehow. At home in Lidköping it was merely empty, dead. A chasm constantly threatening to swallow her.

When she retired, she decided to move back to Orust. Her portion of the inheritance from her parents was almost untouched in the account and would more than pay for a newly renovated cottage with all the amenities, tucked into the forest on the northern end of the island. This way, too, she was a little closer to the only living relative she had, her nephew Bosse, who lived on the outskirts of Gothenburg. He was the only child of her now-deceased older sister, and he and Lilly had once been close, but they'd had only sporadic contact since he became an adult. He was something of a loner, had never had a family or even a long-term relationship, as far as Lilly knew, and alcohol had come to play too great a role in his life. But he was a friendly, kindhearted soul, and she would love to see more of him. The few friends she'd had were all dead.

There was nothing to tie her down anywhere.

The strongest relationship she had was with the beach where she'd lost her son, alongside the sea that had taken him.

✑

There was nothing particularly special about January 11 this year. As usual, when she arrived at the spot, she walked around the area with Lisa for a bit. She typically avoided going by the house where she and Olof had spent those happy years with Johan before it all ended, before the void appeared. Then the dog had to wait in the car while she brought her basket to the bench that had replaced the old stump.

She gazed out at the sea, recalling the sound of Johan's shoes on the rocks.

Today she heard those steps again. The sound of small feet.

She heard steps.

She heard steps.

A boy came pelting down from the house up the hill. He was running so fast, as if he were in a hurry to get somewhere, and he wasn't wearing a coat.

She recognized him. It was the boy from the store, the one who liked to pet Lisa. What was he doing here? Did he live here, in their house? Why was he alone?

He should have noticed her, but he just ran by, down to the water, as if he had no time to lose. When he arrived at the narrow jetty that ran along the rocky wall, he slowed down, approaching the big boulders, his steps now cautious but still determined.

"Hello there," Lilly called. "Hold on."

She stood up, hurried over, and stopped a few meters away from him as he stood on the rocks.

"Come here," she said gently, holding out her hand. "You shouldn't be out there. It's slippery. You could fall in."

He turned toward her, and there was something about his eyes, something peculiar, something she'd seen in her own son's gaze the last night before he disappeared—she remembered it now; it had been so long since she'd thought of it. He had talked in his sleep incoherently, as if he were arguing with someone. Both she and Olof had gone up to check on him, and he had turned to them. His eyes had looked strange, as if he weren't quite there, and she had thought it must be because he was half-asleep.

This boy's eyes were the same.

Then he closed his eyes—and fell backward into the water.

She gasped.

It was as if he had allowed himself to fall.

Lilly stepped onto the big rock, grabbed the ladder with one hand, and caught his sleeve just as he vanished into the depths.

"Sweetheart," she said, mustering all her strength—she didn't know where it came from—and forcing him to climb back up the ladder. In the commotion he kicked off one boot, which sank into the dark water.

"Sweetheart, what are you doing?"

Now he looked perfectly normal, shaken, frightened like a child who had just accidentally fallen into icy water.

She must have imagined that he had let himself fall. She was always imagining one thing and the next; people told her so all the time. And anyway, Johan hadn't done that. Or had he? After all, she hadn't actually seen how he ended up in the water.

She gently led him to the bench, where she wrapped him in the blanket and held him, comforted him.

His scent went through her whole body: his wet hair, his skin, a child's skin again.

"Lisa!" he cried.

He freed himself from her grip and dashed to the car. He didn't seem to care that one of his boots was missing. He opened the door and climbed in to see the dog.

The boy was in her car.

She looked around. No one in sight. Lilly packed the blanket back into the basket, went to the car, and shut the door. Then she got behind the wheel and drove off. She had been planning to go grocery shopping, which she still did at the little country store, where they knew her and where she liked to chat with the staff. But she could just as easily go tomorrow instead.

"I'm glad you got in the car. Your mommy and daddy want me to take care of you for a while," she said. "They called me."

But the boy didn't bat an eye. He just kept playing with Lisa.

She hadn't meant to hurt anyone, of course not. But when she saw the man standing there outside the cottage, staring in at her child, instinct kicked in; she grabbed the first hard object she could find, and hit him. Wouldn't any mother protect her child from what she perceived to be an intruder?

Ever since that woman showed up and rang the bell a few days ago, she had been nervous, full of foreboding that something was going to happen.

She hit the man because she wanted him to disappear. Out of the picture, out of the whole story, out of every part of what she had re-created.

Which he was about to destroy.

Because, of course, she had recognized him.

They'd been so happy together, she and Johan. He certainly hadn't wanted for a thing since he came to her, almost a year ago now.

Naturally, at first she had only meant for him to stay with her for a little while, have some ice cream and listen to a story, and then she would drive him to the police station. She was no kidnapper, but why not give those parents a little scare and let them have a good scolding from the police if they couldn't keep an eye on their child? He should never have been allowed to leave the house all by himself. He hadn't even been properly dressed for the weather. And he didn't know his last name—why, her first Johan had *always* had a note in his pocket with his address and phone number. Not that she ever left him by himself, but you couldn't be too careful as a mother. His parents were lucky that she, Lilly, was the one who had found him.

But he seemed so hungry, poor thing, so maybe he should stay for dinner after all.

That was what she had thought at first. But that was before she understood God's plan.

The first week, he cried himself to sleep every night, calling for his mama and papa until he passed out with exhaustion. She told him that they had to go away for a while, but as time went on, he improved, and after a few weeks he had almost entirely stopped mentioning his parents, his cat, and his Mulle doll. One evening she heard him pretending to talk to his mother on the old cell phone he'd had in his pocket, and the next time she took the car out, she simply threw the phone out the window and into a ditch. Eventually he seemed to have completely forgotten them.

The first time he called her Mama, he seemed to surprise himself; he said it as if in passing, and the word sort of plugged the flow of the other words behind it, but she pretended not to notice. She wanted it to seem natural for him to call her Mama, and from then on it was, and he did—and so did she.

Mama has to go away for a while. You stay here with Lisa. Mama's going to lock the door, but I'll be back soon.

Calling herself Mama again—it was indescribable. The word flowed from her lips like gold, made her shine from within—she could feel it; she could almost see it when she looked in the mirror, how she glowed.

But it wasn't entirely easy to be a single mother, especially not at her age. And she never could have sent him to day care; she'd always felt that if you have children, you ought to stay home and take care of them. Her Johan had never had to spend a single day of his four-year life at day care.

Luckily, Bosse had pitched in on those few occasions when she was forced to be away for a longer period, like the time she went to a friend's funeral in Stockholm last spring, or when she was admitted to the hospital for a few days for a minor operation. The boy liked going to Bosse's; he got to bring Lisa along and loved to look after the rabbits that lived in cages in the backyard.

She'd told Bosse that she frequently stepped in as a baby-sitter for a newly divorced neighbor who had to travel a lot for work until she could find a new job. She asked him to be very discreet when it came to the boy; the neighbor wouldn't have appreciated Lilly, in turn, handing her son off to someone else for days on end. She wasn't entirely convinced that Bosse believed her story, but she knew he would never tell—he was unfailingly loyal to her. And how often did he even talk to anyone else?

She couldn't tell him the truth. He wouldn't understand that God had finally made things right and given her a child back. The sea takes and the sea gives; it was that simple. And who was Lilly to question His decision? Not to mention, if she hadn't been there to fish out the boy when he fell in the water, he'd be dead. Still, she was clear-sighted enough to know that most people were like Bosse, or like Olof, and had little faith; they simply didn't trust in the Lord as she did.

But over the past few months, the boy had occasionally acted out. He didn't like being locked in his room when she had to run an errand, and that was probably what had thrown a wrench in the works. She had noticed the hints of a feeling deep down inside, one that seemed perfectly foreign to her, one that said she was done with him. That she couldn't manage this any longer. But she pushed it aside, figuring that this was just what it felt like to be a parent sometimes—nothing strange about that. And sure, in weak moments she worried about what would happen in the future, when he got older, if something happened to her or if he needed to go to the doctor or the dentist. And shouldn't he go to school? But she quickly dismissed those thoughts, for He took care of His own.

Now she set out into the dark after hurriedly grabbing her coat and car keys. It was time.

She knew as she got in the car that it was all over, but she didn't feel any guilt. Of course not, because she didn't *have* any guilt. She kept her eyes on the endless black sky, and it felt like she was driving straight into it, straight into the gentle darkness, as if all she would ever need was within.

Or in the water, in the murky, redeeming sea that was soon alongside her, how it melted into the sky, into her, into everything around her, how her existence was falling back toward a single, primeval state where everything was still possible but no longer mattered, a restful void, in the presence of God.

She passed the bridges, one after the next, thinking of the accident in the eighties when a ship crashed into one of them, the Tjörn Bridge, in the middle of the night, and the oncoming cars vanished right into the depths, falling head-lights like a string of pearls, and the ship's crew could only watch helplessly from a distance as dreams burst against the surface, and she thought that if that happened now, if the road stopped existing high above the water, if she and the boy drove over the edge and fell into the darkness together, it would be such a perfect ending. If He called them both home. But with that man outside the window, there had been no chance for her to bring Johan along, and all she could do was accept it as fact.

If only she had hit the man harder, bought herself some time.

As she approached a curve before the entrance to the final bridge, she saw the blue lights and signals up ahead, on the other side of the water, on the other end of the bridge.

She made up her mind quickly, if she gave it a thought at all. She felt how the muscles of her right foot tensed, how they cramped, how she pushed the pedal to the floor, how she was driving faster than she'd ever gone before, and the crash as she went through the guard-rail, or maybe she only ran into it and instead the car flew over the top, she didn't know, she knew only that she was flying, that she was spinning uncontrollably, first above the water and then straight into it, as if it were firm ground, a hell of a bang, and then she saw Johan's eyes, she rested within them, she saw how they were so calm and quiet, how they told her, *Everything will be fine, Mama, there's nothing to worry about, this is the end and the end is beautiful, there's nothing more to do back there, nothing more to feel or want or reach.*

It's just the end, Mama, and that's when you wake up.

At first, once Maya had helped Martin come around, he had no idea where he was, or even who he was. He just sat there staring at her, at the house, at their surroundings, until the fog lifted and everything slowly came back to him, bit by bit.

"Maya," he said. "What happened?"

"I think she must have spotted you, the lady, and hit you in the head. There's a random piece of firewood right here next to you. You're going to have quite the goose egg. But she's gone now—I passed her in her car when I got here."

"What are you doing here?"

She smiled. "You called and asked me to come."

"But how did you get here so fast?"

"I already had the address when I got your first message— I've been here before. But let's worry about that later."

He just nodded. Maya helped him get to his feet. She looked at him with an expression he didn't recognize.

314 / SUSANNE JANSSON

Then she asked the strangest question; she said, "Is Adam here?"

"Adam?" Martin repeated. And then he remembered, and said the name again, in a whisper. "Adam?"

Then they turned to the cottage; he looked through the window where he now recalled having seen his son, but where Adam had been sitting it was dark and empty.

"He was inside there," Martin said. "I saw him, for real."

They ran around the house and tried to get in through the front door, but it was locked. Maya called the police and gave them the woman's license-plate number. Martin thought about the firewood: If this woman was desperate enough to attack him because she'd been found out, what would she have done to Adam?

He picked up a rock from the ground and broke the glass pane on the door, then unlocked it and hurtled inside. A small dog came rushing out, barking wildly, and Maya caught it and held it in her arms.

"Adam?"

It was as if he were shouting into a void. As if nothing was there to hear his words, as if he had lost his son once more, yet again, to the void, to the silence.

"Take it easy," Maya said softly, grabbing his arm. "He must be scared to death right now. I'm sure he didn't recognize you when you were standing outside the window in the dark. And you just made a lot of noise, breaking that window and shouting."

But she was speaking to deaf ears. He couldn't stop himself; he dashed around the house, his cries growing weaker until he collapsed in a whimpering heap on the floor. Then he felt Maya's hand on his shoulder, offering gentle encouragement. He turned to her and saw her nod toward the dim room. He spun around and followed her gaze, and there was something there, something moving. A small body detaching itself from the darkness inside.

A boy.

Martin stood up and, for a moment, simply stared at his child. As if all the strength had drained from him.

He approached Adam slowly, sitting down next to him on the floor. He put out a hand, gently touching the boy's arm.

"Hi," he whispered as he wiped away his tears. "Hi, buddy."

A long silence.

"Don't be afraid," said Martin.

Adam didn't say anything.

"Do you recognize me?" Martin asked.

His son looked at him with his bright, penetrating gaze. Then he gave a nod, a quick one. Nothing more.

Martin nodded too, swallowing a sob, a pressure that wanted out.

"Good," he said, his voice almost failing him. "That's really good."

⁓

Alexandra had hardly gotten over the fact that her parents had shown up unannounced for a visit, when the doorbell rang and she found two police officers standing outside.

At first, when she saw them, she thought that she was finally about to get confirmation. That her son was dead, that they had found his body somewhere—in the water, in the best case.

In the water, in the best case.

Dear God, let it be in the water.

She held on to the doorframe and looked at their bodies, saw them losing their shape before her eyes, dissolving.

Their voices faded, leaking out of the realm of her perception.

"Do you understand what we're saying?"

She pulled her robe closed at her throat. "Pardon?"

Then their shapes reassembled before her eyes, and they repeated what they'd said, that all signs indicated that her son had been found alive. That he seemed to be well taken care of.

That he seemed to be fine. That they would take her to see him.

She just stared at them, unable to understand the implications of their words. She asked to get dressed first, and then she followed them unsteadily as her mother and father stayed behind with Nellie.

Just as she was about to climb into the patrol car, a thought came to her.

"Hold on a minute," she requested. "I forgot something."

When she returned, she got in the back seat of the patrol car, and they set off as Maya, on the phone, explained the gist of what had happened.

What if it's not him? Alexandra thought. *What if Martin was confused and made a mistake? What if he's sick again? What if it's some other kid? Maya's never met Adam.*

But then she arrived, and the blue lights were rotating in the dark and the police radio was crackling and the drizzle was falling, and there in the ambulance, it was him.

Adam.

It was her son. A little taller and a little paler than she remembered, but still.

Her Adam.

He was sitting on Martin's lap with a small dog at his feet. She climbed into the ambulance, climbed over to them, was about to fall. She realized that she might frighten him, thought he might think she was a crazy old lady, her face puffy from the pills, her hair stringy, her hands shaking.

So she left some distance between them as she sat down.

"Hi," she whispered. She held out the Mulle doll and saw his face soften.

She moved a little closer, and it seemed to her that she wasn't capable of containing so many emotions, and then she thought of her labor, when she gave birth to Adam after sixteen hours of contractions, and how beforehand she'd expected to sob with distorted happiness once he arrived, but instead she felt a great calm fill her up, a vast and simple joy, and she felt the same thing now, the same unexpected gift; she felt her breathing suddenly grow regular; she felt how she could breathe and speak without the air getting caught in her chest.

"Hi, Adam," she said softly, brushing the hair away from her face. She felt a wide smile breaking through; there was no stopping it. All that existed was this single, great, pure, simple joy, and she became one with it; she became *joy*.

"It's so good to see you again."

Maya packed the last box on top of the folded-down back seat of the car. She hadn't brought much with her when she moved to Orust, and she wasn't taking much now that she was moving back—mostly clothes and computer stuff and photography equipment.

She'd already said goodbye to everyone, everyone but Bäcke. Robert, Lia, Martin, and Alexandra had joined forces to invite her to a farewell dinner at Robert and Lia's last night, and she'd made a particular request not to see them again after that. She hated drawn-out goodbyes.

That was why she was leaving now, at dawn, just as the sun was rising over the water. The best part of the night before had been watching them play together, Adam and Vilgot. As if nothing had happened. As if the months they'd been separated were already forgotten.

Martin had finally told her about his mother, how after her many miscarriages she hadn't been able to take her eyes off him until he was ten years old and a strong swimmer—and hardly even then. Would Martin and Alexandra be the same? Would they ever be able to stop worrying about Adam? Or Nellie, for that matter? Would they be able to feel happy and safe as time went on? No, Maya didn't think they would. Sure, they were planning to move to a house farther inland, but Orust was an island; the sea was never far away.

Maya had remembered to point out to Martin how important it was to clear out the attic before he moved, to throw away everything that revolved around the accidents and the date of January 11. No reason to frighten the new owners. But, of course, the abstract had to be preserved.

She drove along the empty roads, over all the bridges, leaving the sea behind and traveling inland. Toward Dalsland, toward the forest, toward her old life. Her cat, her house, her mother, and her friends.

A tear made its way down her cheek, prompting her to wonder what had happened to her, who she had become in her short time as an islander, in the open, exposed environment there.

She felt a surge of contentment at heading into the darkness again, into the forest, into something that could protect her, envelop her. Or hide her? She'd never felt such a need before, or been conscious of having it.

The house was empty when she arrived; her renter had left the week before and was now off traveling in some warm part of the world. Her friend Ellen, who was the principal at one of the nearby art schools, had promised to light a fire in the woodstove each day and take care of the cat until Maya arrived.

Man Ray came running up to her as soon as she parked the car and stepped out. He meowed and lovingly rubbed himself against her legs.

"Hi, buddy," she whispered. "I missed you."

She looked up at the house, a red two-story Dalsland-style cottage. It looked enormous. Did she really need that much space? She gazed out at the pastures—no cows at the moment. The autumn air was fresh, almost chilly.

Soon October would make way for November.

"Let's go inside," she said to the cat.

⁕

Three weeks after her homecoming, it was time for the opening of the *Winter Water* exhibition in Maya's very own gallery on the first floor of her house. It was the second exhibition she'd had here; for the first she had installed detailed photographs of bog bodies, the remains of people who had been buried in a bog and preserved thanks to the particular biological composition of the ground there.

Now a group of specially invited friends, colleagues, and journalists would see the images she'd been working on most recently. There were fifteen square color photographs, all depicting surfaces of water; they varied widely depending on the weather and the skies reflected in them.

Some were velvety, smooth, and deep black; others were vanishingly pale or powerful, colorful, angry, threatening.

What they all had in common, a review would state a few days later, was that they were captivating to the point of being hypnotic. That you could stand before each of them for a long time, all the while noticing fresh details, different levels of the picture, as if you were being sucked farther and farther in, farther and farther down into the water.

Maya had been thinking a lot about Martin today. This morning she had read in the paper that the sea had flooded Venice again. The water was waist-high on the enormous Piazza San Marco, the heart of the city. There was fear that it might weaken the ground and cause the surrounding buildings to collapse. He hadn't been wrong, that Martin, when he packed his go bag. Perhaps the sea really would drown them all.

Maya typically surrounded herself with lots of people; she was a name, and there was never a shortage of art students or others who wanted to pitch in and help out. But this time she had declined all their help and taken care of the installation on her own, along with Ellen, who had been around part of the time. Now she was standing next to Maya, watching more and more guests come in and help themselves to crackers and sparkling wine.

"It looks great," Ellen said to Maya.

"Thanks. And thanks for your help. It feels good."

"How does it feel to be back? We've hardly had time to talk. About the…personal stuff."

Maya gazed at the floor. "I know."

"You haven't mentioned that guy since you got home. The one you met."

Silence.

"What was his name again?"

Maya looked up and met her friend's eyes.

"Bäcke. He's called Bäcke."

Ellen nodded.

"What happened there?"

"I fucked up," she said harshly, giving Ellen the rundown.

"But," Ellen said, "it doesn't sound like you put all that much effort into convincing him to come back."

Maya glanced skeptically at her friend.

"What? How do you mean?"

A guest interrupted them, and then another, hugging Maya and giving her flowers. Maya thanked them, accepted the gifts, smiling and kissing cheeks.

"But I admitted I was wrong. Isn't that enough?"

"*Enough?*" Ellen snorted. "And that was the best you could come up with?"

"Oh, screw you," Maya whispered out of the corner of her mouth.

Quiet jazz came from the loudspeakers. The room smelled like perfume and flowers.

"Time for me to say a few words," Maya said, climbing onto a chair and tapping her glass.

"I'm especially thrilled to see so many of you here tonight," she said once the buzz had died down, "because, as most of you probably know, I just came home after a period of self-imposed exile. I've spent the last eighteen months in an eco-house in Bohuslän. It's been a very eventful time in a lot of ways, and the nature on the coast made a big impression on me. I've never been properly acquainted with the sea before, and as always, I find the best way to get to know something is through my camera."

She looked out at the smiling, expectant crowd.

"What you see on these walls is the result of that new acquaintance. I don't want to say much more, but I hope you'll approach these photographs with as much of an open mind as possible."

The bells on the door jingled, and when Maya turned to look, she saw some familiar faces. It was Lia and Robert with Jocke and Annika. Maya could tell there was a baby in the carrier on Jocke's belly. Then she saw who was behind them.

Bäcke.

She was almost bowled over. Her body throbbed with a sensation of burning in her chest, stomach, knees.

It was him.

His hair was pulled back in a ponytail, and he was wearing a black jacket.

"So, welcome, everyone," she finally managed to say, "and I hope you have a pleasant evening. We have plenty of bubbly, so don't hold back. Cheers!"

Glasses were held aloft and applause filled the room.

Maya stepped down from the chair and looked at her friend, unable to hide her joy, though it was mixed with nervousness.

"That's him. He came with Lia and Robert and his son and..."

"No way!" Ellen raised her eyebrows but didn't look surprised at all.

Maya was startled; she scrutinized her friend.

"You...?" she said. "Did you...?"

"Go say hi to your guests," Ellen said, pushing her away. "They had a long trip."

Maya patted her hair, took a deep breath, and started their way.

EPILOGUE

I t's perfect," the woman said. "Isn't it?"

"Very nice," the man responded.

They left the house and the real estate agent and walked down to the water. The air was starting to feel really chilly; winter would soon be here. It might even snow this weekend; they said so on the radio earlier today.

But it was nicer to think about warmer weather. Wouldn't it be fantastic to have a place like this by the time summer rolled around? It was not a private beach, but there weren't any other houses close by, so chances seemed good that they'd have the spot to themselves pretty often. The woman imagined the boat they could keep tied up there, a little rowboat. She saw them jumping in for a swim from the dock or the ladder on the big rock farthest out.

This could be their world. It was within reach after all, although she didn't know how many offers there might be on this house. Apparently some have been withdrawn, from what she'd heard, but she didn't know why. All they could do is hope.

The house was an old two-story wood-frame fisherman's cottage. Simple and lovely, nothing spectacular, but that's how she liked it. Windows facing the water, small rooms on the second floor. There was room for another baby. A sibling for their daughter—it was about time now. It'd already been seven years.

Hold on—where was she?

The little girl was standing on a rock and balancing in her rubber boots. She slipped and climbed back up again. Looking out at the water, following the waves as they washed ashore.

Counting them quietly to herself.

One, two, three, four.

A breeze tugged at the bushes, rustling her jacket. Then the girl turned out to face the sea, as if she was listening.

"Hi," she said suddenly.

No one was watching her; no one could wonder.

"Yes, I'm coming," she whispered. "I'm coming soon."

Sometimes, in the winter, when the sea seems to grow deeper and darker, you can hear cries seeking their way to land. Cries, larking and luring.

But perhaps that's just what people say.

Perhaps it's just the wind.

ABOUT THE AUTHOR

Susanne Jansson was born in 1972 in Åmål, Sweden. She later moved to Gothenburg to work in advertising and then to New York to study photography. After returning to Sweden, she spent her professional life combining her work as a photographer with being a freelance journalist focusing on reportage and profile stories in areas such as culture, film, music, and literature. Her debut novel, *The Forbidden Place*, was published in 2017 by Grand Central. *Winter Water* is her second novel.

Susanne Jansson passed away in the summer of 2019 after a courageous fight with cancer.